THE SPIDER:
SATAN'S SHACKLES

THE **MASTER OF MEN!**

SPIDER®

SATAN'S SHACKLES

By Grant Stockbridge

POPULAR PUBLICATIONS • 2022

PUBLISHING HISTORY

"Satan's Shackles" originally appeared in the June 1938 (Vol. 15, No. 1) issue of *The Spider* magazine. Copyright 2022 by Argosy Communications, Inc. All rights reserved.

CHAPTER 1
BORN TO FIGHT

NOT A shirt in the pile had any sparkle or personality. They were all drab—as commonplace as the rack of neckties that hung over the counter. Jackson thumbed through the pile again—and yawned. He was not a Beau Brummel; neither did he covet flashy clothing. But he liked apparel with some originality; and such merchandise was not to be found in Harper's Falls.

Like this little department store, with its two or three clerks, the town was somnolent, down at the heels—an eddy of some twenty thousand souls that had been shunted aside by the fast-moving current of the modern world. The place was quiet, drowsy, almost moribund since the shut-down of the textile mills which were its very heart-beats.

Richard Wentworth had set out to find peace and quiet, a haven in which he and Nita van Sloan would be far from worry and trouble; where the world of crime and violence would be forgotten. He certainly had found it! Jackson sighed. The first week hadn't been bad—but a month of Harper's Falls had him squirming restlessly. For a man who had been tempered on the fiery battlefields of the World War, and then thrust into the perilous vortex of New York's seething underworld, this stagnant little up-state town was a living tomb.

Nothing ever happened in Harper's Falls. Nothing....

During the past week, the local newspaper had been featuring the sensational news of several daring attacks on gas stations and stores—but Jackson almost grinned at this recollection. There wasn't anything in this town worth taking. It had probably been some poor devil so desperate to get out of the place that he had played badman in order to get a stake. The whole town would not be worth the time of a first-class crook....

Jackson finally made an unenthusiastic choice and looked around for a clerk. The two who were in evidence were engaged with customers. Like himself, there were three or four other prospective buyers waiting to be served. A land-office business for Layton's Bazaar, Jackson mused—and subconsciously he

Mad panic reigned as the walls of the school
auditorium crumpled and collapsed!

cocked his ear to the sound of voices coming from the rear of
the store, where the proprietor had his office.

Men's voices were rising excitedly. One was gruff, threatening;
the other quavering and panic-stricken. The customers looked
up inquiringly, as the office door opened and four men surged
out into the store—four men with hard-bitten, cold-eyed faces

strangely out of place in Harper's Falls. After them came gray-haired old Ira Layton, his usually ruddy cheeks mottled with the terror that gleamed from his frightened eyes as he clutched at the arm of one of the men and tried to draw him back.

Jackson's nerves tingled and the blood began to leap in his veins.

"We've never had any trouble here," Layton was protesting nervously. "We aren't like the big cities. We don't need protection—"

"That's what *you* think!" the fellow who seemed to be the leader snarled, and then nodded to the others. "Okay—get busy."

Out of their pockets came large bottles filled with a colorless liquid—bottles which they handled with rubber gloves as they unstoppered them and began splashing the contents over counters, into showcases and wall closets, wherever there was merchandise. At the signal, those pseudo-customers, who had been lounging at the counters, joined the others—and in a matter of seconds the store was being deluged with acid.

"No!" Layton shouted desperately, as he grabbed at one of those bottles. "You can't do that! The police—"

His words ended in a scream of agony as the fiery acid was dashed savagely into his face, to make a flaming hell of his eyes. Brutally, the leader swung on him and smashed a fist into his face. Layton staggered backward, lost his balance, and crashed to the floor at the foot of one of his showcases.

For a fraction of a second there was silence, and then one of the genuine customers leaped forward. A husky, leathery-faced man of about fifty, he sprang at the leader and swung a heavy fist that caught him on the side of the head, spun him backward. With pantherish quickness the old fellow was after the thug, ready to drive home the knock-out blow. Then in mid-stride he stopped short, a look of amazed surprise on his face as he clutched at his breast with gnarled fingers between which the warm blood gushed in a spurting stream.

Before the slitted-eyed killer could swing his automatic to cover the rest of the store, a black hole mushroomed between his eyes, and he toppled over.

THAT SHOT had come from Jackson's gun instinctively, just as the weapon itself had leaped from his shoulder holster into his hand the moment he witnessed the cold-blooded murder. "This isn't your fight—keep out of it!" caution had whispered in his brain. "Remember, you are to keep out of trouble!"

But in that moment his finger was drawing back on the trigger, the ugly-faced leader was toppling to the floor, and Jackson was diving to the protection of a mid-aisle counter as he answered the shots now seeking him from three or four different points.

It happened that quickly.

In a matter of seconds the somnolent store had become a bedlam—an uproar of blasting guns and snarling voices. Vaguely, Jackson glimpsed a girl running down one of the aisles, as his shot brought down the leader. He saw her throw herself to the floor, heard her shrill scream knife through the tumult—then her voice was drowned out by the roar of a gun almost at his ear. Only Jackson's instinctive dive saved him, as the killer's bullet slit a gash through the back of his coat collar.

Then Jackson's gun barked again, and the fellow's exultant curse became a gurgling gasp as a bullet ripped through his throat and pitched him back on his heels. Straight over the fallen man's body, Jackson leaped, his gun blasting right and left.

A howl of agony sounded in front of him, as one of the thugs dropped his gun and clutched at his shoulder. A shout of terror came from one side as another heard death whisper past his ear. Then the acid-throwers were running, tumbling over one another in their eagerness to get out of the doorway. Their discarded bottles broken, or gurgling their contents on the floor, the thugs fled pell-mell, diving low as Jackson's bullets sped them on their way.

Like a thunderous radio program that has been snapped off in mid-scene, that appalling din was hushed, blanketed by a silence which seemed almost unearthly. The silence was broken only by the whimper of a girl's sobs and a low moan of agony. His empty gun still in his taut fingers, Jackson's eyes flashed around the raided store. He saw the bodies of the two thugs he had killed, that of a woman customer who had died almost at his side—and Layton, the proprietor, trying to get to his feet as he clutched at his agony-filled eyes.

Now Jackson remembered his own situation. "The police will be here at any moment," the warning whispered in his brain. "That means questions, explanations—*involving Richard Wentworth and Nita van Sloan....*"

Jackson was already running toward the back of the store, diving low between the aisles as he heard men coming in at the front door. Out he went through a back door that opened on an alley, down its length and came out on a side street. Unconcernedly, although his every nerve was tense, every sense alert, he walked to the corner and turned down the avenue. Two more blocks, and then a glance behind convinced him that he must be reasonably safe from pursuit.

Harper's Falls seemed to be as quiet and sleepy as ever, but now Jackson realized that its outward calm was deceptive. Beneath that appearance of tranquility, trouble was seething—and he had been swept into it despite his pledge to Richard Wentworth to avoid embroilments at any cost....

That thought was still prodding Jackson relentlessly, as he turned in at the gateway of the large Henshaw estate on the edge of town. A month ago, they had come fleeing from New York. Having just put an end to the terror of the Sleeping Death, Richard Wentworth had picked out this remote retreat as an ideal place in which Nita van Sloan might convalesce from the wounds and illness that had almost cost her life.

Mindful of his promise that she should have nothing but peace and rest, Wentworth had engaged the property under the name of John Stafford, shut himself away from the outside world—dropping out of the perilous life of crime-fighting that had so irresistibly attracted him, and severing every connection which might draw him back into it. And now Jackson, his chauffeur and trusted right-hand man, had almost opened wide the fateful door Wentworth had so resolutely closed....

RICHARD WENTWORTH was on the steps of the wide porch, when Jackson walked up the winding drive. He was just handing Nita into the Daimler limousine, where Ram Singh, the tall, bearded Sikh, sat at the wheel—and his deep-set, keen blue-gray eyes were sparkling with satisfaction. He noted the healthy color that had come back in Nita's lovely cheeks, her happy smile and the blissful contentment in the depths of her violet eyes.

For Nita van Sloan this month had been a furlough in Heaven, four weeks of being with Richard Wentworth constantly—relief from fear and worry, a reprieve from the constant dread of not knowing what might be happening to him, of wondering whether he was still alive or had been cut down by a treacherous bullet from the gun of a murderous killer. These four weeks had been a pre-honeymoon, a delicious foretaste of what it would be like to be with him always, secure in the knowledge that his career as a crime-fighter was ended for all time—that, no matter what the temptation, the Spider would not walk again.

Those happy thoughts, so bounteously filling her heart, were mirrored in her eyes as she squeezed his hand and sat back in the car. Wentworth could not fail to recognize and to understand those signs. Release from worry had healed her wounds more than any medicine, he realized. It was rebuilding her, bringing a bloom to her cheeks that thrilled him every time he looked at her.

A few more such weeks and she would be entirely recovered.

Then they would be able to go on to the greater happiness that lay in store—the sunny future he had postponed so often when the sight of suffering, crime-ridden humanity had made him forget his own aims, even his loved one, as he hastened to the defense of those who could not help themselves.

Richard Wentworth smiled at Nita. Then the indulgent lines slowly melted from the flat-planed, vital face that was too strong to be merely handsome—for now he was listening to Jackson's voice.

"I think Miss van Sloan had better wait. There is something I must tell you, sir," Jackson began.

But even before Jackson's lips opened, Wentworth had sensed his message. So perfect was the understanding between these two that he read signals of worry in every line of his faithful friend's face. Nita van Sloan was no slower to understand. Quickly she stepped back out of the limousine and took her place at Wentworth's side.

"There was a bit of trouble in town," Jackson began, and briefly recounted what had occurred. "I don't think there will be any difficulty about it," he finished, "but I thought you should know before Miss van Sloan drives into town."

Now the smile had faded entirely from Wentworth's face. Tall, poised, square-shouldered and perfectly set up, he stood there and listened. His poker face betrayed none of the worry that had flashed into his brain, none of the quick concern for the girl who instinctively pressed closer to him as she recognized the all too familiar storm cloud which suddenly threatened her paradise.

"We were going to avoid situations of that sort, Jackson," he said quietly. "I thought it was our understanding that we were to keep out of trouble, no matter what the provocation."

Jackson squared his shoulders and took it on the chin. But the twinkle in Wentworth's eye and the clasp of his hand took the sting out of his rebuke even before Nita came to Jackson's defense.

"But, Dick—he couldn't stand there and see those helpless people murdered!" she said.

The twinkle in Wentworth's eye became broader, as a glow of warmth stole through him. Nita had every reason to hate violence and fear the approach of trouble. Yet she could not abide injustice, or tolerate criminal ruthlessness, even though interference with them might jeopardize the things she valued most. She was one girl in a million—a hundred million—the only mate in all the world for the Spider, even though he never again unsheathed his deadly guns and took the grim vengeance trail into the peril-studded byways of crime….

Now Wentworth's glow of satisfaction was suddenly chilled. His quick ears had caught a sound in the distance. Keen eyes probing through the trees and shrubbery toward the entrance to the grounds, he suddenly whirled on Jackson.

"Cars coming up the drive," he warned. "They may be after you. Get into hiding quickly. That old trunk in the attic is as good a place as any."

Jackson was already on his way.

WHEN THE two strange sedans drew up at the edge of the drive, Wentworth was just handing Nita van Sloan into the limousine. He looked up in apparent surprise as five policemen and a young woman sprang out and strode toward him. Chief Joseph Skelly, a thick-set elderly man with suspicious eyes and a stubborn, heavy-jowled face, was in the lead.

"We're lookin' for that other driver of yours, Mr. Stafford," he growled, his gaze darting into the limousine and then from window to window of the house. "Not this dark feller—the one I saw drivin' you the other day."

"He's a murderer!" The girl flung herself forward. "A cold-blooded murderer! He killed my father and then ran off with the rest of his gang. But I recognized him! You're hiding him here somewhere, and we're going to get him—"

"You must mean Jackson." Wentworth tried to calm her, but she was beside herself with grief and rage. About twenty, he judged her—a pretty girl in a rough, hard sort of way. "He hasn't come back from town, but I feel sure there must be some mistake—"

"There's no mistake!" she screamed wildly. "I *saw* him do it—shoot my father down! He's in there somewhere, Chief!" She started dragging Skelly toward the porch.

"Guess there's no mistake," Skelly rumbled. "Zella Gorman, here, was an eyewitness. If you're hidin' this man, you better turn him over, Mr. Stafford. Harborin' a fugitive from justice—"

"Perhaps you feel you ought to search the house," Wentworth agreed readily. "I know you have your duty to perform."

Somewhat mollified, Skelly led the way inside and detailed

his men to the search. Wentworth did not leave the front hall, and in a few minutes the officers had returned, to report no sign of the fugitive.

"Well, I guess he ain't here," Skelly conceded reluctantly, as his eyes gave the lower corridor a last suspicious scrutiny. "But I'm not so sure you ain't got him hid out somewhere. I'm warnin' you again—if you try to interfere with us, it'll go hard with you. The minute this feller shows up, it's your duty to report him. Remember that."

Wentworth bridled at the man's surliness and ill-concealed hostility, but he swallowed his irritation and assured Skelly of full cooperation as he followed the police back to their cars. As he drove off, he looked after them thoughtfully—and wondered.

There was something about Skelly's attitude that puzzled him. Not only was the chief unnecessarily hostile, but there was a suggestion of fear in his manner—a frantic eagerness to lay hands on Jackson that transcended mere devotion to duty....

"We have not seen the last of our friend Skelly," he predicted when the police had gone, and Ram Singh had summoned Jackson from his hiding place. "There is something on his mind—and he seems to think that we are the solution. These newspaper stories about hold-ups in the town during the past week, may be running him ragged. Then, again, they may be a part of something far bigger."

He went on. "Ever since we came here there have been radio announcements of troubles of one sort or another in this section of the state—hold-ups, killings, kidnappings, dynamiting, sabotage. Things of that kind are not usual up here. They have all the earmarks of being part of a deliberate criminal campaign—a campaign that has now reached Harper's Falls."

His alert mind was reaching out, putting two and two together, beginning to envision the far-flung ramifications of an organized program of terrorism, and the battle light flared in the depths of his eyes as he felt the quick blood pulsing in his veins. Like a veteran fire-horse, he winded the smoke, tensed to the alarm—but resolutely gripped himself, fighting down the keen desire to leap into the harness. He had expected such temptation.

"Whatever it may be, it is none of our affair," he put an end to the tantalizing speculation. "We are keeping out of it—and the best way to do that is to mind our own business and go along as if nothing has happened. All of us except Jackson." He turned to the chauffeur. "You had better hide out for a day or two until this blows over. Take some provisions and camp in that cabin up on the hill so that you won't be on hand in case the chief decides to pay us a surprise visit. It isn't our fight," he repeated firmly, as if to convince himself, "and we are keeping out of it."

"The master is right," Ram Singh endorsed gravely. "Trouble always can be found by him who seeks it."

"Very good, sir." Jackson nodded contrite agreement and turned to follow old Jenkyns, the butler, out to the kitchen to make up a pack.

For a moment Nita van Sloan looked at Wentworth, and her troubled eyes mutely spoke their gratitude. But her fingers were cold when they closed on his hand. Her lips parted, moved

13

uncertainly—and then were sealed as Wentworth took her into his arms and kissed her.

"I hope—I hope it will be as easy as that, Dick," she said softly when he relinquished her. But the tremor that quivered in her low, rich contralto voice bespoke misgiving—a premonition of evil that would not be denied....

CHAPTER 2
DEATH COMES TO TOWN

NITA SEEMED to have lost all appetite for her usual afternoon drive after that. She started to take off her jacket, but Wentworth quickly protested as he explained the situation.

"It will be better if you go, darling," he urged. "Drive through the town as if nothing had happened. I won't go with you today—I feel it's better for me to be here in case Skelly does return—but they may be watching to see whether your starting out in the car was genuine or only a stall to cover Jackson's getaway."

As soon as she was gone, and Jackson had departed for the comfortable log cabin situated on the hillside about a quarter mile above the main building, Wentworth went back to the living-room and turned on the radio. In a few minutes he tuned in on one of the regular news broadcasts from the station in nearby Holbrook—and again the items had a significant similarity.

Two garages had been raided in Northville, a fire had

destroyed a furniture store in Worden, a mysterious explosion had wrecked a mill in Chauncey, a prominent merchant had disappeared from Haleyville—and storekeepers in Garland were appealing to the police for protection.

"From these reports," the announcer concluded, "it seems that our section of the state is in the grip of an unparalleled crime wave. Police officials, kept busy trying to check the violence within their own jurisdictions, are of the opinion that the menace is more widespread than anything they have ever encountered—a spontaneous criminal outbreak which can only be combated by cooperative action."

Wentworth's blood tingled with the call of battle, as he listened. He sensed something even more far-reaching than those groping police chiefs had begun to suspect. The radio reports of the past few weeks, the news stories in the Harper's Falls daily, and now Jackson's account of the attack on Layton's Bazaar—they all fell into place in a pattern of brazen and deliberate crime whose challenge taunted him.

Indeed, these were no sporadic crimes. Like some poisonous cancer, they were spreading out over the length and breadth of four counties. Behind them undoubtedly was a carefully scheming criminal, a ruthless killer to whom human lives and happiness meant nothing—a cunning scoundrel who laughed scornfully at the fumbling efforts of these small-town policemen trying so desperately to cope with him. This heartless devil should be smashed!

Resolutely, Wentworth snapped off the radio and strode to one of the windows, firmly determined to put the whole matter out of his mind and have no part of it. Too often he had lent a listening ear and become enmeshed before he could stop himself. This time it would be different. This time he would not forget his obligations to Nita, no matter how insistently his own impatient desires might strain at the bit.

At that moment a light tan convertible roadster of sleek design drew up in front of the house and put an end to his thoughts. Out of it stepped a well dressed young woman. Wentworth caught a glimpse of blond hair, small, delicately molded features. Then he was opening the front door, to gaze into a pair of troubled blue eyes that glanced up at him uncertainly, appealingly, from a pale face.

"I am Susan Conant, Mr. Stafford," she introduced herself. "My father is president of the First National Bank of Harper's Falls. It's about him that I want to talk to you, if you can give me a few minutes." Wentworth led her inside, smiled at her reassuringly and did his best to put her at her ease. However her agitation only seemed to increase.

"I'm in trouble, Mr. Stafford." She leaned forward nervously the moment he sat facing her. "I'm so worried that I don't know where to turn. Father has been acting strangely lately—so secretive, so actually *furtive* that he has me terrified. He is afraid of something. The way he looks at me—the way he acts—is frightening. He used to be so full of life; one of the most popular men in town. Now he never goes out. And the only ones who come to see him are queer-looking people who are strangers here in town—people I instinctively distrust."

She took a breath. "This afternoon he has a conference in the

16

Harper House with Willard Kendall, the New York financier, who is here to reorganize the mills. You know about that—"

Wentworth did know about it—as anyone who read an issue of the Harper's Falls *Times* must. For months the local chamber of commerce had been conducting a campaign to interest new capital in reopening the textile mills which had been closed down for nearly two years. At last, it seemed, their efforts were to be crowned with success. Willard Kendall, a well-known New York financier, had been interested sufficiently to come to Harper's Falls, and was staying at the Harper House.

His arrival meant a new lease on life for Harper's Falls. If the proposed reorganization went into effect with Kendall's backing, the bankrupt mills would reopen, business would boom, and a new day would dawn for the all but penniless town.

"I have been following the project." Wentworth nodded at the girl.

"Naturally, my father is deeply interested in the reorganization," she rushed on. "It means a great deal to the bank, and I know that it has been a great strain on him. But that does not account for the fear I have seen in his eyes. He's desperately afraid of something, Mr. Stafford—and I think it has something to do with this reorganization of the mills. That's why I came to you. I want you to help me. I want you to come to the hotel with me now so that you will be on hand if anything should happen."

"But, my dear Miss Conant—" Wentworth looked bewildered—"I don't understand. Why do you come to me—a stranger here in your town? I have nothing to do with this mill reorganization, and I have no right to thrust myself into your father's affairs. Surely you can't expect me to interfere with something that does not remotely concern me—"

"I've come to you because you are the only one who can help me, Mr. *Wentworth!*" Susan Conant hurled her bomb—and then sat staring at him, white-faced and tense. "I know all about you," she said with desperate calm as she unfolded a magazine she clutched with her handbag. "There—you can't deny your own picture!"

THE MAGAZINE which she held out to him was a copy of an illustrated detective story weekly, a publication which featured true crime accounts—and up from the page which she indicated leaped a startling headline, "The Truth about the Sleeping Death—Which the Police Can't Hush Up!" Beneath that shrieking heading was a picture of Richard Wentworth alongside one of Nita van Sloan, and on the opposite page were likenesses of Jackson, Ram Singh and Jenkyns!

Wentworth's eyes narrowed as they skimmed down those columns of damning type. The farther he read the more fully he understood the disaster that had befallen him—the true extent of his helplessness. When his Daimler had sped away from the house in which the diabolical master of the Sleeping Death lay slain at last, Wentworth had hoped and believed that the case was closed. Behind him he had left two witnesses who, having heard the fiend's confession, could explain everything to the police. Now something, it seemed, had gone wrong—terribly wrong.

"When the police arrived at Hulbert Fleming's mansion," the magazine writer had described the case, "they were allowed to enter without opposition, and were then ambushed. Three officers died in the withering hail of lead that poured into them before four of the Sleeping Death's killers darted past them and made a getaway in a car that sped down the street after Richard Wentworth's limousine.

"Dr. George Holden and Nurse Doretta Cahill, left behind to greet the officers, did their best to clear Wentworth and his associates, but their stories were not sufficiently air-tight to convince the smarting police. Chagrined by the bloody finale of the case and the escape of Wentworth, Commissioner Kirkpatrick, who was ordered by his physician to take a rest, left for a month in Europe. In the commissioner's absence, his subordinates have been doing their utmost to pick up the trail which vanished into thin air when the Wentworth car swung around a corner and lost itself in traffic."

The fools! Wentworth cursed under his breath. The poor, blind fools! The evidence had all been left there plain for them to read. But, because some of their men had walked into a trap set by a few of the Sleeping Death's killers, who must have been hiding somewhere in the building, the police had closed their eyes to it and laid the guilt at his own door!

Stanley Kirkpatrick should have had better sense. Once

Wentworth managed to reach him, he knew that he could make the commissioner understand—but Kirkpatrick was in Europe, and his subordinates would be like ravening wolves, eager to score a scoop in his absence.

That meant that Wentworth was still a fugitive from justice. He and Nita must not go back to New York, and were also in imminent danger of being picked up right here in Harper's Falls. Fortunately, the magazine which carried the Sleeping Death article had a very limited circulation. Still, Susan Conant had seen it, and with her the damage was done.

"I haven't said anything to anyone about it," she said nervously when he glanced up and met her gaze. "There were only two other copies of the magazine on the stand, and I bought those. Nobody will know—"

"If I do as you bid me," Wentworth finished bitterly. "And if I decided to refuse—what then?"

"Oh, you can't do that!" she gasped in sudden fright. "You *can't!* I wouldn't want to—" her fingers closed on the magazine, clutched it convulsively—"cause you any trouble. But you are the only man who can protect my father, *and you're going to do it!*"

There was no doubting her sincerity or mistaking her desperation. Wentworth knew that he would be wasting time trying to talk her out of the idea. There was nothing for it but to accom-

RICHARD WENTWORTH •

pany her to the hotel. She could force him to go there. However, she would find it quite another matter to compel him to take any part in her father's troubles, once he arrived there.

"All right," he nodded agreement. "I'll do as you wish."

Before the words had left his lips she was on her feet, holding the door open as she waited impatiently for him to get his hat. Then she went down the steps, took the wheel and kicked the starter, hurriedly.

Wentworth watched her grip the wheel with white-knuckled hands, never taking her gaze from the road. She was quite lovely, and, under other circumstances, probably would have been a very charming companion. Now she was a mere bundle of nerves, keyed up to the breaking-point.

Despite his resentment at her blackmailing tactics, he found himself warming to her, wondering what could be the real cause of her concern. Probably, he told himself, she had imagined most of it. Her father, possibly, was simply abstracted by the importance of the deal he was helping to negotiate. Yet, she did not look like the sort to terrify herself with imaginary bugaboos....

THE MOMENT they stepped into the lobby of the Harper House Wentworth sensed that something was wrong. Danger seemed to permeate the air, to shroud the place like an impalpable veil. He read it in the scared, mask-like face of the clerk behind the desk, the wooden-Indian stance of the bellhop who stared straight ahead of him as if rigid with apprehension. Fear hung recognizably in the silence that made the lobby seem deserted, even though actually half a dozen guests lounged in various corners. But these guests had hard, cold-eyed faces that looked strangely out of place in Harper's Falls.

Wentworth felt a thin, cold tickle traverse the length of his spine, could fairly feel those steely eyes boring into his back the moment it was turned to them.

"Mr. Kendall's suite is on the second floor," Susan Conant said in a scared, choked little voice that was a mere whisper in that oppressive silence. "That is where they are meeting. If we can—"

They had reached the broad staircase, starting up, when her words suddenly died on her lips, clipped short by the roar of shots coming from somewhere above. Like one stricken, she swayed, clutched at the banister, gasped something unintelligible. But Wentworth was already sprinting up the steps.

The sound of those shots had wiped all thought of his peaceful resolve from his mind. In half a dozen strides he was on the upper landing, stood there uncertainly for a moment. Then the sounds of a rough-house battle were unmistakable—crash of tumbling furniture, thud of falling bodies, rasp of cursing voices. Wentworth ran to the door from behind which the uproar sounded. It was locked, and there was no response when he hammered his fists against the panels. Drawing back across the corridor, he hurled himself against the door—again and again—until it tore away from its hinges, crashed inward and catapulted him over it.

Wentworth was halfway across the room before he checked himself against an overturned easy-chair.

Willard Kendall's suite was a wreck. Tables and chairs were broken and scattered as if a giant hand had scrambled them, papers flung over the floor—and in the midst of this litter lay the financier, sprawled on his face, thin fingers digging into the rug that was now crimsoning from the stream of blood that had trickled from his head.

But there was no time to bend over Kendall and investigate his injuries. The instant Wentworth checked his tumbling charge, a gun crashed and lead smashed into the chair beside him. Another bullet cut past his cheek so close that he could fairly feel its hot breath. Then a moan of terror made him swing around to where tall, pompous Herbert Conant now cowered against the wall, holding trembling arms up before his face as a ludicrously ineffective barrier against the flying lead.

"Down on the floor!" Wentworth shouted at him, flashing across the room, crouching and ducking as he leaped to the doorway from which those bullets had come. His own automatics blasted death through the opening, now clearing the way.

The gunmen had just reached the hall door and were running out into the corridor, when he flung himself into the adjoining room. They tried to yank the door closed behind them, but Wentworth's blazing guns drove them headlong toward the stairs. Midway down the flight, he caught one of them, drilled him through the head—the thug teetered for a moment on tiptoes, then crashed down the full length of the remaining steps.

By now the other gunmen had reached the lobby, and Wentworth dodged behind the protection of an ornate balustrade as a shower of lead hungrily sought him. But the killers had given up all idea of further fighting. The one who seemed to be their leader shouted swift orders, and they converged in a headlong dive for the front door. For a brief instant, Wentworth glimpsed that leader's face—and recognized him as one Hilo Flynn, a New York gunman who was distinctly "big time."

Hilo Flynn operating here in poverty-stricken Harper's Falls! That didn't make sense, unless the gangster had picked the small town as a likely place in which to kidnap Willard Kendall...

Those thoughts flashed through Wentworth's mind as he raced down the stairway in pursuit. Across the lobby, out onto the sidewalk, he flattened himself against the doorway just as a last spiteful volley of shots blazed at him.

One of their cars was already speeding down the street, and another got under way before Wentworth could shoot out its tires. One of his bullets shattered the rear window, another *pinged* against a fender—then the car was out of range, and he was standing there in the middle of the sidewalk baffled.

For a moment that scene was like a motion picture still— the astounded passers-by, rooted to the sidewalk, petrified by terror, Wentworth half-crouched above his leveled automatics. A split-second of utter stillness—then he realized that he had been there far too long. Another minute or two would bring the police—Chief Skelly, already suspicious and more than anxious to find an excuse to jail him. Arrest meant questioning, investigation... certain recognition.

Before anyone could attempt to stop him, Wentworth darted back into the hotel, across the lobby and into the bar, where there was an entrance onto a side street.

Police whistles were shrilling behind him when he came through the bar door and raced out. But there was a cross street just ahead, and beyond that an alley which ran behind a garage where he had had the Daimler serviced.

Wentworth roamed through the garage until he located the proprietor at work beneath a car, stopped to talk with him about the price of a valve-grinding job, and then walked casually out the front, where a policeman stood chatting with a taxi driver.

Nodding to the officer, he stepped into the cab and gave the driver his address.

That policeman might serve him as a partial alibi—if an alibi should prove necessary—he considered, as he sat back and watched the excited crowd converging on the Harper House. On the other hand, it was quite possible that he had not been recognized in front of the hotel. He was a stranger in town, and the excited witnesses probably would furnish half a dozen garbled descriptions of him to the police. All except Susan Conant. She knew who he was—and what she might do was problematical....

However, one thing was certain. Harper's Falls was becoming too hot for him and Nita.

Every minute they remained in the town, their jeopardy increased. Swift flight, much as he disliked the idea of running away in the face of trouble, was the only safe course open to them—the only way to avoid jail or worse.

CHAPTER 3
THE ROAD TO RUIN

RAM SINGH'S eyes were bleak and hard as he sat at the wheel of the Daimler, and the thoughts churning through his mind were even more grim than his expression. The scion of a long line of India's fiercest fighters, Ram Singh's great pride had permitted him to bow to no man—until he met Richard Wentworth and recognized in him a man worthy to be called master. Far more than a servant, from the moment he acknowledged his fealty to Wentworth he had given the *sahib* and his lady a worshiping devotion that amounted to idolatry.

With benign approval, Ram Singh had watched Nita recovering health while Wentworth basked in her smiles and yielded himself, for once, unreservedly to the charm of her company. A foretaste of Nirvana, he had regarded that month in Harper's Falls—but now the peaceful idyll was threatened with disruption. Haunting fear had come back into Nita van Sloan's eyes, and Richard Wentworth was worried.

Ram Singh's fingers tightened on the wheel, and a terrible rage surged up within him—the wild, untrammeled desire to maim and kill, to battle savagely against any odds, which had made his Sikh forbears such indomitable fighters. If only he could come to grips with this devil who threatened his master's happiness....

"But the *sahib* has decreed that the path shall be one of peace," his conscience admonished sternly, and Ram Singh put thoughts of blood-shed out of his mind.

Resolutely, he concentrated on the things at hand—the passing scenery, road, car. Then his conscience abruptly flayed him. The gasoline tank was nearly empty. While indulging in forbidden dreams of vengeance, he had been neglecting the duties entrusted to him! He looked around for a filling-station. They were on the outskirts of Harper's Falls, approaching a station which he had patronized on previous occasions. Ram Singh cut down the speed, turned into the curving approach to the pumps—then stepped on the brake, eyes widened in surprise.

Something unusual was going on here. There seemed to be

a fight going on around that
large sedan at the farthest
pump. Before Ram Singh
could bring the Daimler
to a stop, the men around
the sedan leaped into it,
slammed the door; and their
car spurted away from the
station out onto the road.

It had all taken place in a
bewildering rush, but Ram Singh thought he had sensed trouble.
The moment he stepped from his seat he was certain of it. Lying
on the ground beside the farthest pump was one of the station's
helpers, his face streaming blood where he had been brutally
gun-whipped. Clinging to the doorway of the one-room office
and store, a woman was weeping hysterically.

"They've kidnaped him!" she sobbed. "They've taken my
husband—they'll kill him!"

Nita was out of the car and had the woman by the arm,
endeavoring to calm her sufficiently to find out what had
happened. "Who took your husband?" she asked soothingly.

"Those murderers in that car," came bitterly. "He wouldn't pay,
so they grabbed him and dragged him away. They'll take him out
in the woods and beat him until he's nearly dead—just the way
they did to Otto Benisch and a lot of others who wouldn't join
their league. But Phil can't stand it!" Her voice rose hysterically
as she visualized her husband's ordeal. "His heart's weak, and
he'll never be able to stand the whipping! They'll kill him—"

Nita's eyes were flashing, spots of angry red glowing in her pink cheeks as she turned and ran back to the Daimler. "After them, Ram Singh," she commanded. The Sikh hesitated, while his impulse to obey battled with his conscience. Wentworth had said they were to keep out of trouble, and here he was on the verge of plunging the *missie sahib* squarely into it—risking her life against a car full of thugs and killers....

"We can't let them murder that man," Nita's voice lashed at him. "Hurry, Ram Singh!" Now, edged with steel, it was a voice of command like an echo of Richard Wentworth's own.

GRIMLY, RAM SINGH stepped on the gas, and the Daimler picked up speed like a racer leaving the post. The kidnap car had more than a minute's start, but the road was straight and open and he had no difficulty spotting it—little more trouble overhauling it.

Gradually, the powerfully-motored, specially built limousine cut down the distance, crept closer until no more than two hundred yards separated them. Now the quarry knew they were being pursued. Their rear window edged upward, making way for two automatics that nosed through the opening and spat lead at the Daimler.

Ram Singh grinned. This car had been built to stand a far heavier bombardment than those guns could give it. He stepped on the gas in earnest. As if the sedan were standing still, the big limousine swept up, overhauled it, started to pass—then veered sharply in front and started to crowd it from the road.

A howl of terror came from the sedan when the driver realized what was going to happen. Frantically, he clung to his wheel and tried to keep the car from going over, while the thug beside him leaned over his shoulder and drew a bead on Ram Singh's head. His knuckle whitened on the trigger—but before he could complete his squeeze one of the side windows of the limousine shot down—and Nita's gun barked his death sentence.

With a bullet in his brain, he collapsed on top of the driver just as the car rolled into the ditch, pitched wildly, and toppled over on its side with a crash of breaking glass and rending metal.

Out of that twisted wreckage clambered three dazed thugs. For a moment they stood gaping around them bewilderedly. Then the bark of Ram Singh's gun brought them to their senses. Mercilessly, he shot one through the head, then brought down another as the survivors scrambled toward the woods that bordered the road.

The third managed to reach the cover of the trees. Ram Singh followed him for a short distance—then remembered that he had left Nita alone. Regretfully he turned back, and as he went the fellow's snarling voice echoed in his ears.

"You'll get yours for this!" it howled a farewell threat. "You and the dame—" Then it was lost in the distance.

Ram Singh's conscience seized upon the warning and prodded him with it. Wentworth had said that they were to keep out of trouble—and here he had become involved with a gang of kidnapers and murderers! He had killed two, for which he would be a marked man. But, worse, he had let one escape—who could identify him and Nita van Sloan and take their descriptions back to his fellows....

Nita was helping the dazed gasoline station proprietor out

of the wrecked sedan, when Ram Singh's worried eyes discovered her. The man was so terrified that he trembled like a fever victim and could barely stand. But aside from several bruises and cuts he was unhurt. Ram Singh helped him into the limousine and drove back to the station—to deliver him to the arms of his hysterically thankful wife.

The two were still following the Daimler and babbling their eternal gratitude, as Ram Singh resumed the drive homeward—to a meeting for which he had no appetite whatever.

WENTWORTH HAD just arrived at the house. He had dismissed his taxi and walked in to be met by Jenkyns, when the Daimler drove up to the door. He was in the living-room when Nita and Ram Singh entered.

"Trouble, Ram Singh?" He could read it in their faces.

"Truly, master," the Sikh admitted abjectly. "Thy servant has failed to follow orders. On my head be the blame—"

But Nita quickly silenced him. "It wasn't Ram Singh's fault at all, Dick," she interrupted. "He simply followed my orders." She outlined what had occurred.

Wentworth's poker face was stern and uncompromising as he listened, but it was the thought of the danger into which she had recklessly plunged that tightened his jaws. When she finished, a faint smile flitted over his chiseled lips and his eyes twinkled.

"I'm afraid you were not the only ones who disregarded our agreement," he confessed wryly. "I have been in hot water myself—up to my ears." Briefly, he told them of what had happened to him. "The important thing is that at least one person in this town knows our identity. More than likely, there

31

are others. That means we can't risk staying here any longer. We must get out and find another hideout a good many miles from here—the quicker the better." He was frowning a little.

"Pardon me, sir," old Jenkyns interrupted apologetically. "I have been trying to tell you—I had to disregard your instructions, also. Shortly after you left I noticed a man prowling around the grounds, suspiciously. I watched until certain that he was spying on the house—then I put a stop to it."

"You, too, Jenkyns?" Wentworth whistled with surprise.

But the butler was leading the way to a pantry off the dining-room. He opened the door, reached down—and dragged out a bound and gagged man who stared up at them with frightened eyes!

"Good work, Jenkyns." Wentworth knelt beside the fellow and turned him from side to side while exploring his pockets.

A shoulder-holstered revolver, card case and accumulation of personal odds and ends were the result of that search. Wentworth examined them one by one, riffled through the cards in the case and found a dozen printed with the name of August Fricke, private investigator, from the near-by town of Warrenville.

"So you're a private detective, eh, Mr. Fricke?" he commented as he took the gag from the man's mouth. "That's interesting—but I am more interested in knowing who engaged you to come here and spy on me. Who is paying you, Fricke—speak up."

The detective's mouth opened. He started to sputter a denial, then apparently realized the futility and lapsed into stubborn silence. Wentworth pressed him again, and then nodded to Ram

Singh, who was already reaching for the long, razor-sharp knife sheathed at his belt.

One glimpse of that terrible blade was all that was needed to loosen August Fricke's tongue. Words began to pour from him in a frenzied torrent.

"Don't let him cut me!" he howled. "Keep him away from me! I'll talk—I'll tell you anything you want to know. Nathan Henshaw hired me. He told me to keep an eye on you—to find out all that I could about you. That's all I was doing!"

Nathan Henshaw was the elderly owner of the estate, a real estate dealer in Harper's Falls. Wentworth had little use for the man. He had distrusted the close-set eyes, pinched mouth and oily suavity, from the moment they met. But why Henshaw should engage a detective to spy on him was a complete mystery.

"What did Henshaw expect you to find out?" he probed farther. "What are you supposed to report to him, Fricke?"

Terror flared in the detective's eyes as that wicked-looking knife moved suggestively closer. Perspiration stood out on his face, and he stumbled over his words in his eagerness to reply.

"He wants to know what you're doing—who are you—why you're here in his house. He doesn't believe you. He thinks—"

At that moment came the reprieve for which the fellow must have been praying. Outside there was the sound of brakes, cars coming to a halt, men's voices.

Wentworth tensed, listening, then cat-footed to one of the curtained front windows. Again there were two cars out in the drive—from which half a dozen uniformed men were climbing.

33

Again, Chief Skelly led them to the steps. But this time it was Herbert Conant, the banker, who strode at his side!

Herbert Conant... did that mean that his daughter had divulged Wentworth's identity? Or was he there simply because he had recognized "John Stafford" in those hectic moments in the Harper House? There was no time to investigate that now—time for nothing except flight. Wentworth whirled on Nita and the others.

"The car!" he ordered. "We can still make it out back."

He hurriedly led the way to the rear door, stepped out warily onto the back stoop and then held the door open for Nita. Ram Singh darted past them, raced to the big double garage, and in another moment the Daimler's powerful motor was humming. Silently, the car glided out into the drive.

The police were pounding on the front door, demanding admittance as Wentworth helped Nita into the car. They were running around the house now, but he scrambled in after Jenkyns—and then the limousine was under way, a dark streak that hurtled past the outraged officers. Shouts of rage pursued them, as ineffective as the hastily aimed bullets. From the rear window Wentworth saw the police clambering into their cars. But even if the officers had had a fair start, the Daimler would have left them far behind before they reached the edge of town.

Getting away was the simplest part of Wentworth's problem. But now he could not flee from Harper's Falls, because Jackson was left behind, hiding out in the summer cabin and depending on him for protection!

CHAPTER 4
MURDER NEXT DOOR

WENTWORTH'S THOUGHTS millraced, as the car sped along the road. To throw off the pursuit was, of course, most important at the moment. But it was equally urgent that they return to Harper's Falls as quickly as possible—before Jackson was trapped and arrested for a murder he had not committed. Once Chief Skelly laid hands on Jackson, his innocence would avail nothing. Arrest would mean a swiftly framed conviction—if the police did not conveniently leave it to the enraged citizenry to mete out their own mob justice.

Every minute that Wentworth was away from Harper's Falls increased Jackson's peril. Yet it would be folly to try to re-enter the town now in the limousine. The Daimler was a marked car—its description might already have been teletyped ahead to the police of all surrounding towns....

Suddenly, Wentworth picked up the speaking-tube. "Slow down. Ram Singh," he directed. "Take it easy as we approach this next cross-road." Then, "Okay—turn to the right and pass that old farmhouse, slowly."

Face close to the window, Wentworth studied the ancient, weather-beaten building that stood some hundred feet off the dirt road. As he had suspected, it was empty, windows broken, shutters sagging and hanging from one hinge, front door probably stolen for firewood. The discolored *For Sale* sign had long since lost all hope of attracting possible buyers to this old ruin.

But behind the house was the thing which had first caught

35

Wentworth's eye—a large barn partly hidden by tall maples. An ideal hiding place for the Daimler, if there was nobody watching the property.

"Drive in this side-road," he ordered. "Up there behind that clump of trees. I want to have a look at this place."

Like much country property, the barn was in much better condition than the house. The door was held shut by a rusty padlock that fell to pieces at the second blow, and the inside was almost empty. Carefully Wentworth reconnoitered the buildings, but there was no evidence that anybody had been near the place for months. At his signal, Ram Singh drove the car inside, and the paint-scaled door was drawn shut behind it.

"Nita, I want you to stay here with Ram Singh and Jenkyns." Wentworth quickly outlined his plan as he took a make-up kit from one of the Daimler's many compartments and went to work on his face. "I am going to hitch-hike to Weston and shop there for another car. I'll pick up a second-hand sedan and a lot of baggage. When I come back for you, we'll put on Indiana plates and go back to Harper's Falls as a party of tourists."

"Ram Singh—" he eyed the impassive Sikh regretfully—"I'm afraid you will have to sacrifice your beard. Trim it short and close. Your turban will have to go, too—every man and youngster in Harper's Falls will be on the lookout for it. Blacken your face and put on a suit of livery. You are going to be a Negro chauffeur for a while."

Then, his own face transformed so that he seemed to have aged at least ten years, and his immaculate clothing changed for a ready-made suit that was none too well fitting, Wentworth hurried back to the main road and started plodding toward the next town.

TWO HOURS later, he was back at the wheel of a six-year-old Cadillac touring car, its right running-board and rear piled high with strapped-down suitcases that looked as old as the car. Quickly, he sorted through the secret compartments of the Daimler, selecting a supply of guns and ammunition, another change of clothing and other items which he might need before he could return to the limousine.

"All right, 'Tom.'" He grinned at Ram Singh. "That's your name now, you know. Don't forget that you are driving for Frederick Baker, of Kokomo, Indiana—in case we are questioned. Understand?"

But nobody seemed to give them a second glance when they drove into Harper's Falls and parked on one of the main streets. The town was still buzzing with excitement over the events of the afternoon, and the evening daily had devoted its entire front page to the most startling news that had broken in Harper's Falls within the editor's memory.

"Willard Kendall Attacked by New York Racketeers!" the headline screamed. "Attempted Kidnaping Thwarted by Police!"

Following that was a detailed account of the outrageous attack on the financier. As he read, Wentworth learned that the attack had come just as Willard Kendall and Herbert Conant were sitting down for a conference. Kendall had been so seriously injured that his personal physician, who always traveled with him, was in constant attendance at his bedside and refused to permit him to be removed from his suite to the hospital. Heavily bandaged and in great pain from the beating he had received while resisting the kidnapers, Kendall had been seen by reporters but was too weak to be interviewed.

The kidnapers, the article continued, had made their escape after two of their number had been killed. But their leader had been recognized by Herbert Conant as the John Stafford who had been living in the Nathan Henshaw house for the past month—and who had also been reliably identified as a New York racketeer and fugitive from justice!

"Conant's daughter must have talked," Wentworth muttered grimly. "Either that or someone else has seen that magazine article. They are no doubt checking now, and tomorrow our faces will be spread all over this sheet."

"But Conant knew that it was you, and not the police, who drove off the thugs and killed two of them," Nita puzzled. "Why hasn't he said that? Why is he so vindictive against you? Do you know?"

"He was so terrified that he might have believed anything." Wentworth gave the banker the benefit of the doubt. "He didn't actually see me shoot those two, and, when a town is as jittery as this one, people are likely to jump at any conclusion."

Harper's Falls *was* jittery. The paper featured an appeal to the local business men from Clifford Brackett, the executive secretary of the chamber of commerce, prominently boxed on its front page. "Don't be stampeded!" he tried to rally them. "Harper's Falls is on the threshold of a new prosperity. Realizing that, a ruthless gang of thieves and murderers has descended upon us, determined to terrify us into submission and force us to accept racket rule. If we give in now, we are licked and might as well close up shop—every dollar that flows into the town will be sucked from us by these human leeches. Our only hope is to stick together and resist determinedly. Together, we can put up such a fight that these criminals will be glad to scurry back to the big cities where they find easier pickings!"

Wentworth had received a call from Clifford Brackett, soon after renting the Henshaw place. A vigorous young fellow of the go-getter type, Brackett had come to Harper's Falls about a year ago, highly recommended for his organizing ability. His enthusiasm had injected new life into the sleepy chamber of commerce. It had been his efforts which were largely responsible for interesting Willard Kendall in reopening the mills—only to have this trouble break out just as he seemed to be within reach of success....

But that was Brackett's problem. Wentworth's, at present, was to find living quarters as quickly as possible.

Turning to the classified columns, he checked off half a dozen "To Let" propositions which sounded possible. The third in the list proved to be about what they needed—the lower half of a two-family house in the poorer section of town. Furnished and rented by the week, it was in a neighborhood where transient tenants were taken for granted and subjected to little surveil-

lance. Wentworth engaged it and put the car in the ramshackle garage at its rear. Then, while Ram Singh and Jenkyns stayed with Nita, he set out to look for Jackson.

THERE WAS no evidence of a police guard, when he reached the Henshaw estate, but he entered the grounds warily. He worked his way cautiously through the shrubbery until he had a

Back and forth into the ruins, Wentworth
plunged to rescue trapped victims!

clear view of the house. It was entirely dark, but he gave it a wide berth and circled until he reached the faint path that led up to the summer cabin.

Ears attuned for the slightest suspicious sound, he froze the instant he thought he heard a stirring in the dry leaves, the snapping of a twig. Long minutes he poised there, every sense quickened, right hand on the butt of a holstered automatic. But there was nothing but the faint murmur of the wind among the trees, the distant drone of a night insect.

Convinced that he had been mistaken, Wentworth went on until the cabin loomed ahead of him, a darker splotch in the little clearing that surrounded it. Not a glimmer of light came from its windows. That must mean that Jackson wasn't there, that he was searching for his friends somewhere in the town—or that the police had trapped and jailed him!

But perhaps he had been able to leave a note or a message of some sort inside….

Wentworth whistled softly as he stepped into the clearing, then called Jackson's name. There was no answer, not a sound, at first. Then came a dull thumping, banging—and a strangled groan!

Gun in one hand, pocket flashlight in the other, Wentworth ran to the door and flung it open. Then he snapped the beam of light into the living-room—full onto the bound and gagged figure of Jackson threshing frantically on the floor. Jackson was tied hand and foot, and had been lashed to a couch. But he had managed to jerk his bound feet loose and throw his body off onto the floor. Helplessly, he dangled by his wrists while he chewed at the gag and tugged at the rope viciously cutting through his skin and trickling blood down his arms.

Quickly, Wentworth untied him and cut the gag loose. But it was minutes before Jackson could regain control of his tortured jaws.

"Henshaw," he managed to gasp at last, "he tied me up. Look out for him—he may be back." Then, while Wentworth helped massage the circulation back into his tingling limbs, he said quickly, "I heard the shouts and saw the Daimler run past the police, so I worked my way down close to the house to see what was going on. Mayor Estabrook joined the police and Conant, a little while after you left. Then two others drove up in a car—Arthur Deckle, the editor of the *Times*, and the man who owns the Harper House—Atwood, I think is his name."

He took a breath. "They went all over the house and then had a powwow in front of the garage. I could see that they were greatly agitated, so I crept up as close as I dared. I was just beginning to make out their voices when a club came down over my head and knocked me out. When I recovered my senses, old Henshaw had me by the collar and was dragging me back here to the cabin. He tied me up and then started to question and threaten me. He wanted to know who we really are, what you are doing in Harper's Falls—and also asked me about a fellow named Morley."

Jackson rubbed one leg. "When he saw that he was getting nowhere, he gagged me and told me I'd stay here until I talked—or until I rotted. That must have been a couple hours ago—"

"Henshaw," Wentworth mused. "First, he hires a detective, then he starts gumshoeing on his own." He frowned a bit.

"He acted nervous as a cat," Jackson added. "He threatened and blustered a lot—but beneath that I could see that he was plain scared. Same with the rest of those old fellows—something has gotten under their skins good and proper."

Cautiously, Wentworth led the way out into the clearing, but again the night was absolutely still. Not a sound but the careful tread of their own feet—until suddenly something landed heavily on Wentworth's back. Instantly, he doubled up so that his head almost touched the ground, and his assailant sailed through the air and thudded against a tree. Then Wentworth was after him, lashing fists into his face.

Behind, he heard Jackson grunt with satisfaction as his own fist smashed into the face of another attacker. Wildly, they groped and struggled in the almost stygian darkness. Wentworth drove his man back, heard the fellow panting—then felt him tear loose, diving into the brush, just as a flashlight momentarily revealed Jackson's battle-grim face.

Instantly, that flash winked out, and then they were alone—the sound of blundering footsteps fading in the distance as their assailants took to their heels.

"I wonder if that was more of our friend Henshaw's work," Wentworth puzzled, after he had led the way by little frequented back streets to the hideout where Nita and the others awaited them. "What I can't understand is why he is so anxious to know who we are. It can't be that he has discovered that Sleeping Death write-up, for then he would know our identity without the necessity of spying."

"Probably he has heard some inkling of it and smells a chance to grab reward money," Nita suggested. "That may be why he is so secretive, trying to keep anyone else from cutting in on him."

"And that may be why that light was flashed in my face," Jackson nodded. "If he got hold of a copy of the magazine—"

None of them heard the finish of that sentence. Jackson's words were drowned out by a terrific explosion that rattled the windowpanes and sent two loose ones tinkling to the floor—a blast that shook the whole house and echoed hollowly in their ears. Wide-eyed, they stared at one another. There came another thunderous detonation, then two more in quick succession.

WENTWORTH WAS the first to recover his presence of mind. Quickly, he snapped off the lights and led the way out to the front stoop. Still stunned by the sudden bombardment, the few people who were on the street cowered back in terror. But now windows were opening on every side and heads were popping out—to stare down the block where greedy flames were beginning to lick up the side of a wrecked building.

That building was a large dairy, Wentworth saw as he ran toward the still sagging and splintering ruin. The entire front had been blown away, and part of the roof was caved in. From half a dozen spots, flames were leaping up through the clouds of dust and smoke. Incendiary flames, without a doubt! And after

45

the first hush that followed the appalling crashes, the screams of human agony were unmistakable!

Out of a pile of wreckage struggled the bloody figure of a man, who groped for a few blind steps, then fell back into the maze of snapped-off timbers and crazily strewn debris. God only knew how many more like him were imprisoned in the trap that was quickly becoming a blazing Inferno—innocent victims doomed to horrible death!

Recklessly, Wentworth leaped into the sagging wreckage, watching his footing like a log-rider as he made his way to that fallen wretch. All his strength was required to pull aside the timbers that had already settled over the prostrate body as if deliberately to complete his diabolical doom. The man was unconscious, but Wentworth managed to get the limp body to his shoulders and stagger out through the choking dust to where others relieved him of his burden.

Then Wentworth went back into the chaos, warily treading between death-traps that yawned for him on every side. Half a dozen or more bleeding bodies he snatched from the hell reaching out for them. How many were there he did not know. Horror had numbed his mind—horror and a bitter, all-consuming hatred for the callous monster who had ruthlessly doomed these unsuspecting workmen, condemning them to frightful agony and oblivion so that his own criminal purposes might be accomplished!

For fiends like this there could be no place on the clean earth! Like poisonous reptiles, they must be stamped underfoot, ground into the dust until there was an end to them and their kind!

Now others were helping Wentworth. The street was crowded with onlookers, and the more courageous ventured into the death-trap. Hundreds of eyes were turned on him as he staggered out with another victim. But now smoke and grime had contributed to his make-up so that there was no chance that he would be recognized. He was safe. But Jackson, who toiled nobly beside him, wore no disguise, Jackson….

Wentworth blinked the dust out of his eyes and squinted. Yes, he had not been mistaken—that was the girl, Zella Gorman, there in the crowd. For a moment, she had been looking straight at Jackson. Surely she must have recognized him! But at that instant a scream of agony located another trapped sufferer whom the flames had reached. Wentworth doggedly battled his way to the rescue, although the hot flames were singeing his clothing, bathing his body with sweat, his aching lungs so dust-clogged that he could scarcely breathe.

Somehow, he managed to get the trapped man free, drag him to safety. Dizzy and weak-kneed, he swayed on his feet before plunging back into that livid hell. Then Nita's arms closed around him, and Ram Singh, on his other side, drew him back.

"You have done enough, Dick," Nita pleaded. "If you go back in there again, I'll go with you! The police are here now. They will do whatever can still be done."

Reluctantly, he let them lead him away from that blazing hell into the cool night air that filled his grateful lungs. Now Jackson had joined them. Wordlessly, their minds too crammed with horror to permit conversation, they walked down the block to their hideout—and almost into the arms of Death!

WENTWORTH'S KEEN eyes were all that saved them. They had almost reached the house when he thought he caught a flicker of light against one of the windows. It was probably nothing but a reflection from the blazing dairy. Yet it might have been the reflected gleam of a match held to a cigarette; a match in the hand of a waiting—

"Down!" he snapped, as he detected something moving in the deep shadows.

Leaping in front of Nita, he blasted a shot at that moving skulker. A howl of pain echoed it—and then guns simultaneously blazed at them from every side—across the street, the doorway of the house next door, the dark driveway leading to the garage—that semicircle of gun fire would have commanded the stoop to their house and turned it into a death-trap the moment they set foot upon it!

Crouched on the sidewalk, Wentworth's guns fired at the flashes, blotting out two of them. Beside him, Ram Singh's gun was roaring, and Jackson was cursing softly because he had no weapon. Another howl of pain from the darkness, a gurgling scream—and Wentworth leaped up to charge. Instantly, the door of the house opened, and a man from the apartment upstairs stood silhouetted against the hall light. Before he could leap back inside a bullet slapped him backward, to sprawl, lifeless, over the threshold.

Wentworth's guns cut down the murderer, as he tried to break for cover. Then he was blasting shots after two others who took to their heels in panic. They dived around a corner… and again an almost palpable silence settled over the feebly lighted street.

The trap had failed, but now another was closing upon the intended victims. That gunfire had attracted plenty of attention. People were turning away from the burning dairy, peering down the street. Out of the lighted hallway came a woman from the upper apartment. She stood aghast over the body of her husband and then threw herself, screaming wildly, upon him!

Police whistles shrilled. Men came running. In another minute the house would be surrounded by a gaping crowd. As a hideout, it was now worthless.

Holding Nita's arm, Wentworth reached the garage. He tugged open the creaking doors, as Ram Singh ran inside and flung himself behind the wheel of the car. As he backed it out into the driveway, the street end was already spotted with figures. A policeman came running up, to peer into the darkness as he went for his gun.

"Right through them, Ram Singh," Wentworth ordered tightly. "Jam down on the horn."

With the siren screaming, the car lurched forward, roared through the driveway and careened into the street. On two wheels it turned, the squealing of skidding tires mingling with the rattle of shots that whipped after it… and then it was in the clear, streaking into the night before any other machine could give chase.

CHAPTER 5
THE SPIDER'S BROOD

WHO WAS responsible for that deadly ambush? Was it Zella Gorman, who had recognized Jackson at the dairy? Or was it the thugs who had turned a light on his face in the woods above the Henshaw place? Wentworth did not know. But very evidently he and his party were not wanted in Harper's Falls—neither by the police or the gangsters who were holding carnival there. Everyone seemed anxious to speed them on their way—as he, himself, wanted to do.

Yet this was like running away—from those poor unfortunates who had perished in the dairy, the blameless victim who had been murdered on his own doorstep. Did they not ask for vengeance?

It was a decision which Wentworth, alone, could make. He waited until they were well out of town and then told Ram Singh to draw up at the side of the road.

"We are pretty well in the clear," he said while the others regarded him inquiringly. "We can go on to any town we pick out—any town but Harper's Falls. What is going on back there is none of our affair. When we might have helped them, they tried to jail us. Now—"

"Now we are leaving a lot of helpless country people at the mercy of a gang of vicious criminals," Nita finished his sentence. Her face was pale and tense, but her eyes flashed angrily. "It isn't right, Dick—no matter how important it is that we keep out of

50

trouble. When I think of that poor woman standing over the body of her husband—"

"But you are far from strong yet, darling," Wentworth reminded her. "You need at least another month of peaceful convalescence."

His eyes turned to Ram Singh, and the Sikh nodded gravely. Jenkyns murmured dutifully. "You are quite right, sir." Then Wentworth looked at Jackson. Grim-faced, still begrimed from the dairy holocaust, the chauffeur nodded also. "It's none of our fight," he agreed tonelessly.

"In this I cannot make the decision for all of us," Wentworth told them simply. "All our lives are at stake. The decision is for each of you to make." Out of his pocket, he had taken a paper of matches and an envelope. Now, with a grim smile, he tore off five of the matches and distributed them. "Tear your match in half. The bottom half means we go on our way. The top half—with the head—means that we go back to Harper's Falls. Here's the ballot-box." He held the opened envelope to receive their votes.

Despite his self-control, Wentworth's palm was damp as he emptied the envelope into it. He opened his fingers—and stared at five match-halves, each tipped with a blue head!

Wordlessly, he looked from one to the other. Deep down within him pride and genuine affection glowed with a comforting warmth. In that moment he knew that this ballot had been a mere formality, its result never in doubt. These four were the Spider's brood—loyalty and courage bred in their bones. No matter what their heads might counsel, their hearts would never

Through the entire newspaper
plant murder-mad thugs were
wrecking everything in sight!

let them turn their backs on fellow men who so desperately needed their aid!

"We have only about fifteen hundred dollars left," he reported the common exchequer which was in his keeping. "From now on we may be split up, so I am going to divide the money evenly. You, Ram Singh and Jenkyns, will stay with Miss van Sloan. Better take a few rooms in an inconspicuous, second-rate hotel on the west side of town—the Warwick will be all right. Register under assumed names—James Cameron and his daughter, Hazel. Ram Singh will be your colored chauffeur. Jackson and I seem to be the trouble magnets. It's too dangerous for us to be with you, but we'll keep in touch with you. We'll disguise ourselves as unemployed mill hands and take a room in one of the River Street boarding-houses."

On the edge of town, the two shabby looking pseudo-mill hands got out of the car. With a farewell squeeze of Nita's hand, Wentworth led the way toward the river, watching until he found an old red brick building with a "room to let" sign pasted on the side of the doorway. The dingy room they hired was dismal, the narrow beds were hard and bumpy—but almost as soon as their weary bodies touched the sheets they fell asleep.

Wentworth was up early the next morning and went out scouting for out-of-town papers.

AS HE expected, the news from neighboring towns indicated that Harper's Falls was not alone in its troubles. Steadily, the list of outrages increased—fires, robberies, sabotage, kidnappings and beatings; all the shabby, underhanded tricks of the racketeer fastening his talons into the vitals of helpless industry. But none of these was as bad as the reign of terror now raging in Harper's Falls. Wentworth could not understand this, for the town was of little importance, after all.

Compared with a dozen of its neighbors in the surrounding

counties, Harper's Falls was decidedly third or fourth rate. If, as he suspected, a wide-spread drive was in progress to shackle the up-state cities and place them under racketeer domination, it was surprising that this little town should be picked out for such marked attention....

Back in the boarding-house room, he and Jackson reviewed the trouble from its start, puzzling over every possible lead.

"Nathan Henshaw is the best bet," Wentworth decided. "There are several questions he may be able to answer. I want to hear him explain his sudden interest in my identity."

Again they walked across town to the secluded estate that had been their home for the past month. Again, as they scouted warily through the grounds, there seemed to be nobody on guard, the house deserted and closed up. Approaching it carefully, Wentworth sidled up to the back door. His hand had no more than touched the knob, when he stiffened.

It was the sound of shots—coming from somewhere up the hill! Now he glimpsed a plume of smoke rising above the tree-tops at just about the spot where the summer cabin should be!

With Jackson at his side, he started up the slope on a run. But just as they approached the clearing, he yanked the chauffeur back into the protection of the trees—and probably thereby saved his life. Bullets whistled over their heads and thudded into the shielding tree-trunks, as three gunmen raced from the burning cabin and dived into the woods.

Wentworth's own lead streaked after them. But there was no time to be lost if he was to get into that cabin before it became a huge bonfire. Pushing in the door, he crouched low to avoid the cloud of smoke that billowed out at him. Then he was inside, blurring eyes darting about the living-room, seeking some reason for this deviltry.

He found it!

Slumped in a chair beside an overturned writing-table was fat, blubbery-featured old Nathan Henshaw. The top of his bald head was horribly gashed with wounds from which blood ran down into his face, soaking his shirt. He seemed to be dead, but when Wentworth shook him he saw that a spark of life still lingered in the huge body. Henshaw's heavy-lidded eyes opened slowly—filled with the fear of death.

"Clem Morley," he managed to gasp. "Clem Morley—he did what he said… He come back an' killed me—"

His voice dribbled off into a choked whisper. Wentworth bent closer. He tried to make out the words, pressing the dying man with more questions. Henshaw seemed to hear, to understand. His close-set eyes opened again, already glazing. His voice came thickly.

"Herb Conant… He and Morley…" Desperately, he tried to finish, but the frantic light sank back farther and farther in his eyes—then winked out entirely.

Wentworth dropped down on his knees alongside the dead man's chair to avoid the smoke which was thick in the upper half of the room. His hands searched among the scattered papers that had fallen from the table when it turned over. Sheets of writing paper, they were ink-stained, blood-spattered. All were blank—except one that had slid beneath a chair. This one seemed to be a half-finished letter.

Wentworth blinked his watering eyes, as he snatched it up and peered at it. It was addressed to—Richard Wentworth!

"I am desperately in need of help," it read. "My life is in the gravest danger, but if a man like you will help me I may have a chance. Please don't turn down this appeal, I beg you. I will pay you anything you ask, anything I have if—"

That was all. The writing trailed off into a widening blot, and Henshaw's blood sprinkled it with periods. That frantic appeal for aid had been written too late....

Jackson had been doing his best to fight the blaze, but the water supply was inadequate. Now the smoke was so thick that Wentworth's head swam and he could barely crawl to the door and drag himself outside. Clem Morley—the name kept ringing through his brain. Clem Morley had been here and done this. Clem Morley must be the one Henshaw had feared, the one against whom he was so anxious to get help.

But *who* was Clem Morley?

ALL THE rest of that day, Wentworth and Jackson tried to find the answer to that question. All afternoon they haunted the town's bars, talking with bartenders and unemployed mill hands. But nobody seemed to have heard of a Clem Morley.

By nightfall, Morley's identity was still an enigma—but the identity of "John Stafford" and his "accomplices" was emblazoned for all of Harper's Falls to read. Featured on the front page of the *Times* was an expose of their masquerade illustrated with reproductions of the photographs that had appeared in the magazine article!

"Now we'll probably have the New York police up here hunting for us, too," Jackson muttered softly, as he stared down at his own likeness.

Wentworth scarcely heard him. Another voice was ringing in his ears—a voice that vaguely stirred a responsive chord in his memory. Casually, he glanced up from the paper—and spotted Hilo Flynn, the New York killer, at the farther end of the bar. Flynn was with another individual who also had the ineradicable stamp of the East Side slums upon him.

It was fully an hour before the gangsters left. But when they did depart Wentworth was close on their heels, Jackson was waiting across the street. Through the almost deserted factory section of town, the trail led; past the last rooming-houses and saloons, to the very doors of the dark mills—then right into one of the closed buildings!

Those mills, Wentworth knew, were under the control of Herbert Conant's bank, which held a mortgage on them. The bank was supposed to maintain watchmen to guard them—yet these out-of-town thugs had walked up to one of the employees' entrances and entered without challenge.

Something was wrong. Either the watchman in this building had been disabled, or....

At that moment, the door opened again. Wentworth glimpsed another hard-faced thug who came out and took his post near the entrance—a sentinel replacing the watchman who should have been on duty. Quickly, Wentworth signaled to Jackson and then, when the chauffeur crept up beside him, outlined a plan that had been forming in his mind.

Jackson nodded his understanding, whispered a word of

caution. Then Wentworth began working his way closer to that shadow-hidden door and its watchful guardian. Closer... now he dared go no farther. Tight against the wall, he flicked a pebble from his thumbnail—a pebble that bounced out on the street.

Almost immediately, he caught a snatch of tuneless humming, a snickering laugh, then another burst of discordant song as an unsteady figure came swaying down the sidewalk and turned in at the mill gate.

"What the hell?" the sentry gritted savagely, as he catfooted out of the darkness. "You know damn well—"

With a leap, Wentworth was upon him, bringing a gun barrel down over his skull before he had time to cry out. Then Jackson had hold of him, jamming a gag into his mouth and ripping off his belt to wrap it securely around his wrists. Before the guard could do more than groan he was trussed up helplessly, dragged far back into the darkness and left there while Jackson took his place at the door.

Cautiously, Wentworth opened that door and stepped inside. He was in a passageway—a corridor that led to the spinning rooms. A single electric light burned halfway down its length. From somewhere beyond it came the hum of voices. Softly, he walked down the corridor until he could see a door at its end. If he opened that door, he might bring Flynn and his whole gang down on him—but that had to be risked.

Inching it open with infinite care, he found himself looking into one of the big spinning rooms. A light was burning in the center, but its weak beams did not reach the door. With more confidence, he pushed it open until he could wedge his way through. He closed it soundlessly behind him, and clung to the shadows cast by the looms as he worked his way carefully toward where a dozen or more men were sitting and talking.

THERE WERE nearly a score of them, Wentworth discovered—thugs and killers from the gutters of Manhattan's underworld. Arranged in the open space between two double rows of looms was a line of army cots strewn with bedding and odds and ends of clothing. Beyond all doubt, this was the barracks of the gangsters who had been terrorizing the town—the hideout the police had not been able to find.

Among those evil countenances he recognized several of the thugs who had figured in the attack on Willard Kendall—Kendall, whose reopening of the mills would have routed these rats out of their nest…That must be the reason he had been attacked and beaten up so badly—so that he would not be able to interfere until these devils had had time to accomplish whatever evil purpose brought them to Harper's Falls!

"They're running around in circles," he heard Flynn chuckle as he answered a question from one of his men. "Now they're blaming everything on this bird Wentworth—and that's jake by me. The paper's full of it." He held up a copy and grinned. "Nice job of printing, ain't it? Too bad we can't let them go on playing with it—but the chief told them to lay off that yapping, and they ain't had sense enough to pull in their horns. They stuck out their neck—and now they're gonna get it."

Gleeful chuckles and guffaws rang through the silent room, and then a dozen of them began asking questions at once.

Wentworth listened attentively. As he caught the drift of

what they were planning, he knew that he had not a moment to lose. Taking advantage of their noise, he worked his way back to the door, slipped into the corridor, and hurried to where Jackson was anxiously waiting for him.

"The *Times* office," he directed, as he led the way out to the street. "We have about an hour to work—or there will be no paper in this town tomorrow."

By the time they reached the newspaper office, Jackson had been informed exactly what part he must play in their plan. Wentworth stepped into the office first and asked to see the editor. But his cheap clothing and unkempt appearance were against him. Two secretaries rose to bar his way, and a uniformed guard started forward heavily—until suddenly all three were staring into the muzzles of a pair of automatics.

"Back against the wall," Jackson ordered softly, as he disarmed this guard. "Stand there quietly and nobody will be hurt."

Wentworth was already past the gate, striding across the general office to the private compartment lettered with the name of Arthur Deckle. Without announcement, he opened the door and confronted the thin-faced, gray-haired publisher.

The moment Deckle saw his unexpected visitor, he made a dive for one of the desk drawers. Wentworth was on him like a flash, pushing him back into his chair and appropriating the revolver the publisher had almost reached. Fearfully, the old man slumped back in his chair. He was white-faced, haggard-eyed, as if waiting to hear his death sentence.

"Nothing is going to happen to you, Deckle," Wentworth tried to reassure him. "Nothing at all. I simply want a little information that you haven't been printing in your paper. Where is Clem Morley, and what do you know about him?"

Deckle's Adam's apple bobbed up in his thin throat and strangling noises came from half-opened lips. Instinctively, his hand flashed to his inside coat pocket, from which the edge of a wallet barely protruded. Then he regained control of himself. His face became a stony mask, lips clamped tightly shut.

"Morley murdered Nathan Henshaw this morning because Henshaw took too long to answer that question," Wentworth said grimly. "You still have a chance to save yourself, Deckle."

"Morley—did that?" the publisher gasped despite himself.

"You may be next—unless Morley is stopped," Wentworth reminded.

"Yes—he must be stopped!" Deckle could not get the words out fast enough. "He will kill us all, unless we—"

Too late Wentworth heard the tell-tale squeak. Throwing himself to one side, he whirled around—but the roar of a .38 caliber revolver thundered in the little office. Arthur Deckle's words ended in a thin scream, as he half-rose to his feet. Then he collapsed over his desk. The door at the farther end, that had opened no more than an inch, now snapped shut again—a key turning in its lock. Deckle, too, had decided to talk too late....

AS IF that death-blasting shot was a signal, bedlam seemed to break loose all through the building before the echo had faded. The crackle of pistol fire, raucous chatter of tommy-guns, deep boom of explosions rocked the building—all blended into a nightmare of noise and wild confusion.

Leaning over the dead publisher, Wentworth reached into

his pocket. He grabbed the wallet, which had seemed to worry Deckle the moment he heard Clem Morley's name. Thrusting the wallet into his own pocket, Wentworth ran out into the main office. Jackson had now thrust his captives behind desks, and stood ready to defend them fiercely.

All through the three-story plant, murder-mad thugs were driving the terrified workers before them, smashing presses, upsetting type, cold-bloodedly cutting down anyone who dared make a stand or was not fast enough in getting away.

This was even worse than Wentworth had anticipated. But why had the attack come so soon? That could not have been the plan... Then he saw a face he recognized—that of the sentinel who had been posted outside the mill. He understood now. The bound man had been found and liberated and his discovery by the thugs had hastened their attack!

This senseless slaughter was ghastly, appalling—the work of men who had become beasts. Wentworth's blood boiled. Hot rage urged him to fling himself upon the killers, but an iron control held him back—guiding him instead, into a small office that was wrecked.

Out onto a desk-top came his ever-present makeup kit. He propped a mirror up against a telephone—then his flying fingers busily began transforming his face into a thing of repulsive ugliness. Sallow skin, haggard and lined with deep wrinkles; glittering eyes gleamed out of cavernous sockets; snaggly teeth protruded from an almost lipless mouth; bushy brows and long, matted hair hung around his head like the tattered remnants of a shroud—all of this combined to create an apparition of fearful menace.

From beneath his vest he brought out a black slouch hat with a floppy brim. From the lining of his coat came a long black cape that covered him from head to foot. Leaping back through that office doorway, the twisted, stooping figure of the Spider now flung himself into the battle!

With a burst of wild, maniacal laughter, he swooped down upon the startled killers, his blazing guns blasting a path before him. Howling in terror, the raiders broke and ran for cover—only to find their Nemesis seemingly all around them, his guns seeking them no matter where they fled.

"Grab those guns in the hands of the dead rats!" he screamed to the terrified workmen hiding among the machines. "Now follow me!"

A foreman leaped out and snatched up a gun; one of his men followed him, then another. With shouts of fresh courage, the workmen rallied behind the Spider and followed him from department to department, driving the disorganized, fleeing killers before them. In a very few minutes the building had been recaptured... or what was left of it.

Great holes were torn in the floors and walls where dynamite had shattered them. The big presses were tangled heaps of wreckage, the linotypes battered into junk, the type cases upset and their contents scattered in every direction. The voice of the press was stilled—but, Wentworth vowed grimly, another voice would take its place!

In a corner of the vandalized pressroom, he stripped off the dark habiliments and the ugly visage of the Spider. Tearing a six-foot long sheet of paper from one of the great rolls, he spread it out on the floor and went to work with a can of red ink and a brush.

As he had finished, he nodded with hard-lipped satisfaction.

When the curious townsfolk gathered in the morning to gape at the wrecked *Times* building, they would find, posted up outside, a crimson proclamation. It was an obituary for Editor Deckle, and a solemn promise that his work would be carried on by the Spider—whose blood-red insignia was its nightmare!

CHAPTER 6
SEALED LIPS

S UNDAY IN a small town is always a day of peace and quiet, but when Richard Wentworth came downstairs the next morning Harper's Falls was like a city of the dead. Terrified by the rapid succession of outrages, the people were keeping off the streets. Not a store was open, and even the hotel lobbies were deserted as if nobody any longer trusted his fellows sufficiently to dare mingle with them.

Again Wentworth pressed his inquiries about Clem Morley. But now the trail seemed to have run out completely. Whenever he was able to start a conversation, the response was always the same—nobody had ever heard of Clem Morley. Yet now Wentworth knew that he was on the right track. Somewhere, somehow, Morley was at the bottom of this reign of terror.

In the wallet taken from Arthur Deckle's pocket, he had

found a note from the mysterious Clem. It bore a Harper's Falls postmark, and simply said, "It has been a long time, but I have not forgotten—nor will you! Clem Morley."

The nebulous Morley must be in town, even though nobody would admit knowing of his existence. Nobody? The police should know! Yet Wentworth hardly dared trust his disguise on them. They were arresting suspicious or inquisitive strangers on sight. But if he could not go to the police, then maybe to the mayor....

But when Wentworth telephoned the mayor's home, a servant told him that Estabrook was in a conference at the city hall. That conference could be for no other purpose that to devise means of combatting the scourge now prostrating the town—and Wentworth wanted to have a hand in it.

Quickly, he considered the possibilities—then reached a decision. "If they really want to know how to stop this thing, I'll tell them. Jackson, I'm going to sit in on that conference."

But when they approached the city hall they saw that precautions had been taken to exclude uninvited participants. Two burly policemen, revolvers strapped outside their coats, stood at the top of the short flight of stone steps, barring the door.

"The letter trick," Wentworth directed—and instantly Jackson fumbled in his coat pocket, brought out a crumpled note and studied it as if puzzled.

Suddenly spying the officers, he started up the steps and held out the piece of paper with a request for directions. Both policemen reached for it—and before they realized what had happened they were backing away from a pair of leveled automatics. One was in Jackson's hand, the other in Wentworth's. He came sprinting up the steps apparently from nowhere.

"Inside, gentlemen," Wentworth ordered softly, and the stunned officers made no attempt to resist.

Once inside, they were quickly disarmed, gagged, and trussed up with their own handcuffs and belts. Then Wentworth and Jackson dragged them into an empty office, left them there. While Jackson remained on guard just inside the front door, Wentworth went up the stairs to the second floor. He tiptoed from door to door until he located the mayor's office, heard the buzz of voices behind it.

THERE WERE four men in that conference, when Wentworth unceremoniously joined them—four elderly men, haggard and badly worried. Mayor Estabrook, Chief Skelly, Herbert Conant and George Atwood, proprietor of the Harper House, were the four. Startled and wide-eyed, for a moment they were glued to their chairs, their faces blanching with terror. Then Skelly went for his gun—only to sink back like a deflating balloon when the black muzzle of an automatic abruptly lined on his flinching stomach.

"Keep your seats, gentlemen," Wentworth ordered. "All that I want is your attention. You did not invite me to this conference, so I had to invite myself—*because you need me.* I see you do not recognize me, though you have all been very busy identifying me the past two days."

Chief Skelly started. His eyebrows arched, lips half-opened— and a trace of a smile flitted for a moment over Wentworth's face.

"You *are* keen, chief," he acknowledged. "Yes, I am Richard

Wentworth—the John Stafford who has lived among you for the past month. I am here to offer you my services—those of an experienced criminal-fighter—in this hour of Harper's Falls greatest need. I know the sort of people you are fighting."

"Of course you do—they're your own gang!" Skelly blustered. "You come here, raise hell in our town an' then have the gall to force your way into this meeting!"

But the mayor was pounding his fist on the conference table, demanding silence. Conant sat in his chair, stiff as a ramrod. Hell, itself, seemed to be raging in the depths of the banker's unblinking eyes. Atwood was literally quaking with terror and looking as if he would gladly have given his last dollar to be anywhere but here.

Four badly scared old men… but Wentworth set about reassuring them and winning their confidence. Simply, he told them about himself and his experience. Briefly, he narrated the story of the battle with the Sleeping Death; and as he talked the effect of his simple, straightforward recital began to have its effect. The fear began to fade from their eyes, and he could see that now they were convinced that he was innocent of the New York charges. Also, they were convinced that he really could help them—and this was the opportunity toward which he was working.

"Gentlemen, if you want me to clear the thugs out of your town and put an end to these outrages," he suddenly hurled at them, *"tell me what you know about Clem Morley!"*

Instantly, they froze. He could see their lips clamping shut, terror flaring back into their eyes. Only Atwood tried to speak.

Half a dozen words trembled from his lips—then he subsided under the terrified glares of the others.

"Morley is in this town," Wentworth bit off his words grimly. "He is behind this criminal outbreak. Nathan Henshaw knew it—that's why he started to write me this note before he was murdered." Onto the center of the table, he flung Henshaw's blood-spattered plea. "Arthur Deckle knew it—that's why he gave me this threat." The Morley note was spread beside Henshaw's.

As if staring at their own death warrants, the four conferees riveted their eyes on those ominous scraps of paper. Then, as one man, they began to protest that they knew nothing whatever of Clem Morley. They denied it with a vehemence eloquent of the dread in their hearts.

"Very well, gentlemen," Wentworth eyed them challengingly. "You will not cooperate with me, but I ask that at least you do nothing to hinder me. I have been retained in this case by a dead man—" he nodded to Henshaw's unfinished plea—"and I am staying in until it is finished."

"You have my word on that," Mayor Estabrook nodded agreement. "Unless we find evidence that you actually are directing this gang of criminals, no attempt will be made to molest you. If we knew where we could locate you—"

Wentworth eyed them one by one—then told them the name under which he was living and his address. Putting the notes, which were his only tangible clues, back into his wallet, he started to leave. Then a door at the opposite side of the office opened to admit Clifford Brackett, the chamber of commerce

69

secretary. Brackett looked at him in surprise as he dropped into a chair beside Mayor Estabrook at the conference table. Wentworth wondered about him.

He questioned Jackson as soon as he got downstairs. "Where did Brackett come from?"

"He was in the building when we arrived," Jackson said with sudden concern. "He came downstairs with Susan Conant a few minutes after you went up. He took her to the door and then went back up again. I didn't know whether to stop him—I figured you must have seen him."

Wentworth wondered how long Brackett had been standing outside that door; how much the secretary had overheard before he stepped in to join the conference….

THAT QUESTION became even more significant that evening, when Wentworth and Jackson came home to their lodging house. As they climbed the stairs to their floor a drunk was reeling along the hall ahead of them. Swaying unsteadily, he caromed from wall to wall, finally brought up in front of their door. Foggily, he groped for the knob, turned it—then toppled forward as the door surprisingly opened for him.

For an instant, he teetered on the threshold. Then there was a blinding flash and an explosion that seemed to tear the ancient building to pieces!

Wentworth and Jackson were knocked flat by that blast, hurled back halfway down the corridor. Staggering to their feet, they saw that what had been the doorway of their room was now a gaping hole, still drizzling broken plaster onto the splintered beams of the torn-up floor. Door and doorway were blown to matchwood, the walls were a wreck—and the bibulous roomer had become a ghastly thing of disembodied limbs and torso so frightfully mangled as hardly to resemble anything human!

Providentially for them, he had stepped into a death-trap which had been calculated to eliminate them most effectively. That trap had been set by someone who not only knew their identities but also where to locate them. By Mayor Estabrook, Chief Skelly, Herbert Conant, George Atwood—or by Cliff Brackett?

Wentworth pondered that question as he and Jackson got out of the wrecked building and mingled with the crowd already thronging the street. If one of those five was guilty, he undoubtedly would have taken ample precautions to conceal his tracks. The only chance of uncovering him now seemed to lie in gaining the confidence of his hired killers—in working back to him through Hilo Flynn!

Wentworth had met Flynn—but not as Richard Wentworth. More than once, he had stood at a felon-patronized East Side bar with the gunman. But on those occasions all trace of Richard Wentworth had been lost in a slovenly, frowzy-faced, shambling personality the New York underworld knew as Blinky McQuade, safe-cracker and ex-convict. It was for the benefit of such acquaintances—so that he might penetrate criminal rendezvous where only the initiate might enter—that Wentworth had conceived Blinky McQuade and brought him into being. Here was a chance for Blinky's disguise to serve once more, even though hundreds of miles from the congested slums which were his natural world!

But it must be a one-man job. Despite Jackson's protests, Wentworth insisted on leaving him. He directed him to take a room in another lodging-house, arranging to meet him later that night. Then Wentworth went out to the Daimler. A compartment behind the rear seat yielded a pair of metal-hooded glasses and threadbare suit, powder for turning his black hair to an indifferent gray and mouth pads which twisted his face and gave his lower lip a slack droop.

A shambling, round-shouldered nondescript hanger-on of the underworld, Blinky McQuade locked up the barn and started shuffling down the road to Harper's Falls until a truck picked him up and supplied him with a hitch-hike the rest of the way.

GETTING INTO Hilo Flynn's mill barracks was not difficult—if a visitor did not mind going in at the point of a gun. Blinky shambled up to the side door, started to open it inquisitively—and a guard at once was at his side, grinding a hard automatic muzzle into his ribs.

"What the hell!" Wentworth snarled as he half-turned. "Some day someone's gonna burn you down when you pull a stunt like that, young feller. This is Hilo Flynn's hangout, ain't it? How do I get in?"

"That's just what I'm gonna show you," the sentinel jeered, and his mean little eyes looked over Blinky contemptuously. "Get goin'."

Down the corridor and into the spinning-room the automatic muzzle jabbed the way. Once more the place was crowded with thugs—but more so than on the night before. Hilo was sprawled on a cot, watching a card game being played on the floor.

"Visitor callin' on you, Hilo." The guard grinned as he thrust his captive forward.

Flynn looked up eagerly—but showed no recognition. His interest faded, gave way to a mean glint in his cold eyes. "Who is the mug?" he demanded.

"Hell—you know me, Hilo," Wentworth wheeled as he pressed forward into the light. "Blinky McQuade—from Balmy's. I seen you there lots o' times—there an' at China Sam's."

"Maybe so," Flynn admitted. "Lots of guys see me—but that don't mean nothing. Who are you and what the hell are you doing horning your way in here?"

Now his nasty temper was rising. He sat up on the cot and stared at the cringing Blinky, suspiciously.

"I'm right," Wentworth protested. "I heard you was here so I come in to see if I could join up. I'm right, I tell you, Hilo—" as Flynn started to rise threateningly. "You know Shorty Longe or Shark Donahue or Monte Blitz? They c'n okay me. I know Joe Schroeder an' Tony Crucci," he rushed on as the gunman's sneer widened. "Pete Schwieder—"

At last he had struck a familiar name! Hilo Flynn's eyebrows raised, and he looked Blinky over as if seeing him for the first time.

"So you know Pete Schwieder, eh?" he said with wolfish satisfaction. "Well, we'll soon find out whether you're lying about that. Pete is up here with us—over in Warrenville. I've got a man going over there tonight, and you can trot along an' pay Pete a visit. While you're waiting, I'll make sure you won't get lost."

He nodded to several of his thugs, and Blinky was seized and securely tied, hand and foot. Trussed up helplessly, they dragged him to one side, propping him against one of the looms.

For a moment things had looked bad, and Wentworth had been on the verge of going for his guns. But hitting upon Pete Schwieder's name had given him a respite. How successful this would be remained to be seen—for his acquaintance with Schwieder was little closer than with Flynn. At least, now there would be time to think over a plan.

His busy thoughts came to an amazed stop when the corridor door opened and the sentinel escorted in a new visitor—who proved to be Herbert Conant, the banker!

Conant was ill at ease. Wentworth saw him eying the ring of thugs, nervously. Conant's face showed relief when Flynn came up and shook hands. For several minutes, they talked in low tones, and then Conant turned to leave. But again the man seemed uncertain, afraid to leave this wolf pack without mollifying them.

"I am sorry you men have been disappointed this way," he addressed them haltingly. "We—er—expected to have the mills operating by this time, as you know. The—er—attack on Willard Kendall has set us back. But I am sure the delay is nearly over, and we shall be able to put you to work. Meanwhile, I have left some—er—money with your foreman to purchase additional supplies."

He was talking to those thieves and murderers as if they were honest mill workers waiting for jobs! What was the man—an utter fool or a hypocritical rogue? Was that money he had paid them—blood money? Payment for the dynamiting of the dairy and the murderous raid on the *Times* office?

The moment Hilo Flynn escorted Conant to the door, the thugs eyed one another with knowing grins and chuckles. A sarcastic remark about their "supplies" brought a gale of derisive laughter. But before Wentworth could fathom the meaning of what he had witnessed, Flynn was back in the doorway—was calling to two of his men to get the captive started on his way to Warrenville.

CHAPTER 7
BAIT FOR THE WOLVES

JACKSON PACED the corner nervously and glanced up and down the dark street. He took another look at his watch. Wentworth had told him to check in at a rooming-house and then come to this corner. That had been at seven o'clock, and now it was after ten. For the past two hours Jackson had been alternating between a restaurant on one corner and a tavern on the other, always keeping his eyes on the street. As the minutes passed, his apprehension increased.

He had not liked the idea of Wentworth's sticking his head into the lion's mouth by going into Hilo Flynn's gangster head-quarters—but Wentworth had overruled him. Now there seemed to be nothing to do about it—except wait. Or had he already waited too long?

Back once more in the tavern, Jackson stared over the glass of beer that stood on the bar in front of him, wondering what to do. Should he stay here and wait longer or go to the factory and take up his vigil outside the entrance the gangsters used? Should he try to get by the guard and follow Wentworth inside?

Suddenly, his unseeing eyes came back to the barroom and focused on a face at the other end of the bar. That face cut through his abstraction, tugged at his memory. Zella Gorman! It was the girl who had accused him of killing her father and had almost had him jailed.

She looked straight at him but did not recognize him, turned back to the beer she was sipping. Jackson thought quickly. Finding her here might prove to be a godsend—if the plan, now rapidly taking shape in his mind, would only work....

Patiently, he waited for her to leave the tavern. She seemed to have no idea of going. The beer stood before her endlessly—and the minutes were speeding by that might be fraught with deadly peril for Richard Wentworth. At last Jackson could wait no longer. He would have to gamble at making his own opportunity. Walking into the back room, he stayed there a few minutes, then went back to the bar—suddenly stepped up to the rail beside her.

"You are Zella Gorman," he said softly, after the bartender had set up another beer and turned to wait on a customer. "I know you, and you know me. My name is Jackson."

Her eyes widened and she seemed about to scream. But his low command stopped her—that and the hard something that jammed against her arm from beneath his coat.

"That's right." He nodded. "It's a gun. I don't want to use it on you—but don't make a squawk."

Zella Gorman wasn't the squawking kind. A mill girl, brought up in the poorer section of town, she knew how to take care of herself without shouting for help. Her eyes narrowed, lip curling contemptuously.

"All right—what do you want?" Her voice was as low as his.

"I want to talk to you," Jackson said. "Not in here—outside. Finish that beer and walk out the way you usually do."

Without a word, she obeyed. Hard on her heels, he followed into the street—and instantly had a wildcat on his hands. Scorning the threat of his gun, she threw herself upon him, scratching and kicking, jabbing her fingers into his face, clawing at his eyes.

Handicapped by the gun, Jackson was almost knocked down before he could holster it. Then his arms closed around her, held tightly so that her hands could not get loose. Her face was pressed against his coat to prevent a scream. Every second counted. Momentarily, someone might come along, take her part or shout for help.

"Listen," he begged, as he forced her down the block away from the tavern door, "I'm not going to hurt you. I just want to talk to you. You think I killed your father, but I didn't. I tried to save him from the thugs who shot him. You hear that?" He shook her, and made her listen. "I didn't kill your father—but I can take you to the men who did."

Twice he repeated that, and at last she seemed impressed. Her furious struggles ceased, and she looked searchingly into his eyes as he reminded her of the set-up that day in Layton's Bazaar.

NITA VAN SLOAN

"I didn't actually see you shoot him," she admitted then. "I saw the gun in your hand—saw you shooting and running. But if you know who killed my old man, I want to see him. If you're not lying, come along with me, and I'll take a chance on you."

ZELLA GORMAN led the way to a ramshackle tenement where she summoned two young huskies, Lon and Chick Owens. They regarded Jackson suspiciously and listened skeptically to his story.

"Yuh say these fellers are in one o' the mills? Well, suppose we trail down there an' have a look at them." Lon made the decision; and Jackson led the way, an alert guard close at each side.

The mill street was dark and deserted when they turned into

it. Now the Owens brothers picked the route and carefully worked their way toward the building Jackson indicated. When they were within a hundred feet of its gate—suddenly an automobile turned into the street. For an instant, its headlights flashed upon them, seemed to reveal them starkly. Then it went past. They pressed close against a building, as they watched it slow down—finally stop in front of the gate for which they were headed.

Out of that car stepped Herbert Conant!

Zella Gorman's fingers clutched Jackson's arm. Her eyes were wide with surprise. But she made no sound as she watched the banker glance nervously around him, then dart through the gate toward the employees' entrance at the side of the mill.

"Herb Conant!" she whispered, after he had disappeared in the darkness. "What do you suppose he's doing down here?"

Five minutes later, she had her answer. Conant reappeared, two lithe, pantherish strangers escorting him to his car and opening the door for him. As the cowl light illumined their smirking, evil-looking faces, she barely repressed a gasp.

"That slick-looking devil with the pasted down hair—he was one of the gang in Layton's when Pop was killed!" she muttered the moment the car had disappeared and the thugs gone back

79

through the gate. "So *those* are the weavers Herb Conant was supposed to bring to town—dirty murderers like himself!"

NITA VAN SLOAN stood behind a curtained window in the Warwick Hotel and stared down into the empty street. It almost seemed to her that this quiet town was a steel-jawed trap, closing relentlessly around her. The Sunday afternoon calm was deceptive, like a bland mask covering a menacing devil-face. She had been out that morning, passed the ruins of the dynamited dairy. She had read the Spider's grim promise posted outside the wrecked newspaper office. Now she was wondering where Richard Wentworth was, what he was doing. Was he safe, or did he need her?

Often, she had believed herself inured to things of this sort. She had steeled herself to have confidence in Wentworth's ability to take care of himself. But each time, when she actually knew that he was again staking his life against the ruthless cunning of those to whom human life meant nothing, her reaction was the same. She was nothing more than a woman—loving her man, heart and soul.

Terror sat in many a home in Harper's Falls that day, but the women in those homes at least had their men close beside them. To them the terror was an abstract thing hanging over the town. To her it was so close, so personal, threatening at every moment to snatch away all that made life worth living.

Wentworth had telephoned that morning that he dared not come for fear of bringing trouble down upon her. Since then, she had been trying to think of some way in which she could help him, share and lessen his peril. Surely, there must be something she could do, some part to play....

The sound of a key in the door whirled her around. But it was only old Jenkyns, coming in from a walk around the town. Nita noticed that his face was grave, eyes troubled.

"You haven't seen him?" she asked quickly. "There isn't anything the matter?"

"No—it's not that." Jenkyns shook his head quickly, and then the frown deepened between his eyes. "There is nothing that I can put my finger on. But something about the way the people in this hotel look at me makes me feel that we are under suspicion, Miss van Sloan."

"I know, Jenkyns," Nita nodded. "I have felt it, too. Perhaps it is only our imaginations—we are penned up here with nothing to do. Yet there must be *something* we can do, Jenkyns. This is my fight as well as Dick's—I voted to take a part in it. I can't stand much more of this endless waiting!"

"I have a suggestion," Jenkyns ventured, and Nita saw that his shrewd old eyes were kindling with excitement. "There is a cigar and stationery store about three blocks from here where I have been stopping for papers. I questioned the proprietor about his business this afternoon. He is pathetically anxious to sell out. Of course, that is not unusual in Harper's Falls today—it seems that every other merchant has sold his place or is trying to market it. But this man is so eager to get away that he will accept almost any offer."

He went on. "It occurred to me that by pooling our capital we could buy him out." Jenkyns hesitated and glanced from Nita to Ram Singh. "In that way," he pointed out, "we could get out of this hotel and into less public quarters. At the same time we would be angling for a contact with these racketeers who are terrorizing the storekeepers."

"Excellent, Jenkyns!" Nita quickly endorsed. Her eager mind was leaping ahead of him, visualizing that "contact" they would make with the racketeers, seeing in it the opportunity to aid Wentworth that she had been seeking!

Half an hour later, "James Cameron" and his daughter called on the shopkeeper, and before they left they had agreed to purchase the store complete with the furnished rooms at its rear. The next morning they took possession, as soon as the proprietor could get to his safe deposit vault in the bank and have the sale completed. Then Nita started making preparations to receive their expected callers.

THE FIRST request to see the new proprietor came early in the afternoon. The visitor, instead of being the hard-eyed, bullying thug Nita expected, was a pretty, anxious-eyed young woman.

"So you are the man who snatched my store away from me!" she pretended to pout when Nita called Jenkyns and introduced him as the new owner. "I can't understand what possessed Mr. Carmichael to dispose of it without waiting for me. I fully intended to buy him out and had made all arrangements. I know it probably sounds foolish—but I *want* this store, Mr. Cameron. How much do you want to sell it to me?"

Jenkyns shook his head and smiled. He told her that he was not interested in selling.

"But you *must!*" the girl burst forth impulsively. "Surely it can't matter to you—one store is like another! This one means so much to me! I'll pay you whatever you ask—the price doesn't matter." She began again, as she saw that Jenkyns gave no indication of changing his mind. "Surely you can't refuse me!" Her blue eyes were nearly frantic, brimming with tears as her lips started to twitch.

That was enough for Nita. Stepping out from behind the counter, she put an arm around the girl's shoulder, talked to her soothingly. "Tell me about it frankly," she urged, and in a moment was drawing out the story.

"I am Susan Conant," the girl admitted. My father is president of the First National Bank. I just learned that Mr. Carmichael was so anxious to sell this store because the racketeers who are ruining this town gave him until today to meet their demands or take the consequences. That means there will be trouble—for you now instead of for him. I don't *dare* have anything happen to anyone else who is in any way connected with my father or his bank. All morning—" she shuddered—"I have been meeting such hostile, glaring eyes! I have been hearing such nasty rumors about him—"

Suddenly, she seemed to forget what she was saying, and Nita saw that her eyes were wide with surprise. They were staring intently at Jenkyns, dawning recognition in them.

"I know you," she said softly, excitedly. "You are Jenkyns—one of Mr. Wentworth's men! I saw you Friday when I called on him at the Henshaw house. You have changed your face in some way—but I never forget faces, and I recognized your silhouette.

You can tell me where Mr. Wentworth is now. Please, do!" she begged. "He tried to help me before—but now I need him more than ever. Please tell me where I can find him!"

Again Nita appeased her, finally convincing her that they did not know Wentworth's whereabouts.

"I will keep in touch with you," Susan Conant promised as she left. "I'll warn you if I hear any rumor of trouble."

BUT AS the day turned into evening it seemed that her fear of trouble was not to be realized. Night came on, and nobody had attempted to molest the new proprietors. Eight... eight-thirty... nine o'clock—and Jenkyns prepared to close. He brought in the newspaper and magazine stands, then turned to wait on a customer who wanted cigarettes. A mill worker, apparently, Jenkyns noted subconsciously as he counted out change for the dollar the man had given him. Then he turned back to his work.

"Where's the rest of it?" an angry snarl brought him to surprised attention. "That was a five-spot I gave you.

"It couldn't have been, my friend." Jenkyns shook his head, and opened the cash drawer to show that there wasn't a five-dollar bill in it. But instantly he knew that it was no use. One glimpse of the fellow's vicious, slit-eyed face told him that the attack had come!

Warily Jenkyns backed away, just in time to avoid the thug's lunge as he came half-diving over the counter. But now the door was open and others came swarming in—leering ruffians who started upsetting showcases, wrecking counters and shelves. Contemptuously, they ignored Jenkyns and Nita—an old man

84

and a girl—but they had not reckoned with the "colored helper" who suddenly appeared from the rooms at the rear.

Like a charging warrior, Ram Singh leaped upon them, battering skulls right and left with the heavy lilac-wood club with which he had suddenly armed himself. Howls of agony rewarded him as his broken-headed victims fell to the floor or dived wildly out of his path. Those yells were interspersed with shots as revolvers began to bark at him.

With a *"Wah!"* of grim satisfaction, Ram Singh dropped his club. Out from its sheath beneath his belt came the long, bone-handled knife that was his favorite weapon. This knife, once drawn in battle, must never be sheathed again until it had tasted enemy blood. Its keen blade drank its fill in the mêlée that followed. Again and again, it sliced through human flesh. But the odds against him were impossible. Ram Singh was overwhelmed, shot down and left for dead as the savage thugs knocked out Jenkyns and grabbed Nita.

Half-conscious from the manhandling, she was dragged out and thrown into an automobile. The dismantled store had now burst into flames. Brutally, her captors lashed a blindfold over her eyes and nearly choked her to prevent screaming. The car careened wildly through the night… until it seemed to plunge her into hell itself!

Vaguely, she realized that she was dragged from it and down into some kind of cellar, where a score of leering monsters instantly surrounded her. Their chief was a black-robed, hooded devil who stood over her, demanding again and again, *"Where is Wentworth?"*

Nita's senses were reeling, but her jaws locked together determinedly. Frightful spasms of pain coursed through her body as her captors twisted her arms until it seemed as if the bones must snap. They pulled her head backward by the hair, bending her spine in a torturing arc. Fearful agony stabbed up from beneath her fingernails, searing into her arms as red-hot pokers seemed to bore into them. Then at last a wave of soft, soothing blackness swept over her. She felt herself slipping, drifting off into unconsciousness. But just before her senses winked out, she heard the voice of that black-robed fiend ringing in her ears.

"We're wasting time," he snarled. "She's the type who won't talk under any ordinary persuasion. We'll have to give her a taste of the other...."

CHAPTER 8
PUNISHMENT GROVE

S OLLY KLEIN had scant regard for the comfort of his passenger as he drove the small, covered delivery truck to Warrenville. Lying on the hard floor, Blinky McQuade was rolled and tossed with every bump in the road until his whole body was bruised and aching. It seemed an endless trip, but at last the truck drew up among a fleet of disabled cars that filled the quarter-acre lot behind a garage.

"All out," Klein grinned as he opened the rear door and pulled Wentworth to the edge of the car. For a moment he considered. "Maybe I better cut you loose—just in case you *are* a friend of

Pete's. But don't try anything, feller. My rod will be jabbin' your spine, until we get inside. I'd as leave let you have it as not."

His pocket-knife slashed a strand of the rope around Wentworth's ankles, then freed the loops which held his wrists. Wentworth's tingling hands untied the gag and spit it out. Klein now led the way into the garage and downstairs to a large basement room where a dozen thugs circled around a crap game.

Wentworth glanced over them quickly and saw that Pete Schwieder was not here. Moreover, the others did not seem to know when he would return.

"That means we gotta stick around here and wait for him," Klein spat disgustedly. "You can make yourself at home, McQuade—but don't try to pull nothing, I warn you."

Helplessly, Wentworth lounged back in a chair and waited… hour after hour. The crap game broke up. Some of the thugs went to sleep on army cots that lined the walls, while others sat around and talked. But always there were several who kept a wary eye on the dozing McQuade. Long hours of maddening waiting followed, and, as he sat there and tried to plan his next move, Wentworth began to appreciate the magnitude of the criminal organization he was bucking.

From the conversation of his guards, he learned that there was a gang at work "organizing" Warrenville, as there were now in most of the surrounding towns. The "work" was progressing nicely there, with little opposition to the demands of the "cooperative league" from the intimidated merchants.

"There's gonna be even less when the chief finishes putting on his 'demonstration' in Harper's Falls." One of the gangsters grinned at Klein. "That'll take the heart out o' the few wise guys who think they can get away with bucking us."

That league was nothing short of a gigantic extortion scheme which contemplated enslaving the whole state, shackling the merchants of every town and city as it compelled them to pay tribute to their criminal overlords. With his big-city crime methods and organization, this "chief" had been having little trouble riding rough-shod over the small-town businessmen. Also, from the remarks of these underlings, Wentworth gathered that the reign of terror in Harper's Falls was rapidly approaching a climax.

IT WAS not until after dark next day that Pete Schwieder arrived, and Solly Klein came down to the basement quarters to take McQuade up to the local chieftain. Wentworth tensed, nerves cool and ready for any emergency, as he followed the thug to a small office at the back of the garage. But the moment he faced Schwieder he knew that he had lost. The man's little, pig-like eyes flashed recognition—then narrowed to cruel, mocking slits.

"You know me, Pete," Wentworth pretended to fawn ingratiatingly. "You remember when we—"

"Yeah, I know you—you punk," Schwieder sneered. "I remember how you put a bullet in Ricky Davis and left him for the cops to grab and send up the river. I promised Rick I'd square that for him. So guess what's gonna happen to you. You're gonna take a nice little ride—only it won't be back to Harper's Falls!"

Wentworth was weaponless, his automatics taken from him by Hilo Flynn before he was tossed into the truck. Now Klein, assured that he was no friend of Schwieder's, was eying him wolfishly over the barrel of a leveled gun. Every moment was infinitely precious. Schwieder was rising from his desk. Once let him reach the office door, summon the rest of his gang, and Wentworth's fate would be sealed. Schwieder must never reach that door....

"Geez, Pete," the trembling Blinky whined, "you can't do that to me! I couldn't help it about Ricky. He tried to plug me. He—"

Backing away from the threatening gangster, Blinky threw up his right arm as if to ward off a blow—then his hand suddenly whipped into Solly Klein's face as his foot simultaneously snapped back and caught the surprised thug in the groin. Klein doubled up, and steely fingers closed around the barrel of his automatic, wrested it from his half-paralyzed hand. Bellowing with pain and rage, Klein snatched at the lost gun. He tried to ward off the blow that was driving down at his head and crashed through the thin skull beneath his slick-plastered hair.

That brief, deadly struggle had taken only a matter of seconds. Before Pete Schwieder could draw his own gun, he was looking into the blood-smeared barrel of Blinky McQuade's automatic.

"Sit down at that desk," Wentworth ordered in tones that rang with the threat of death. "Write a note to Hilo Flynn. Tell him that Blinky McQuade was a phony—that he killed Solly Klein while trying to make a get-away and then was wiped out by your men. Tell him that the note will be brought to him by one of your men, Lucky Lobin, who will drive back the truck load of supplies Flynn expects."

Pete Schwieder wrote. Disarmed, and with that gory gun

barrel within inches of his ear, he made no slightest attempt to disobey. He was thoroughly intimidated.

"Now you are going out there to the head of the stairs and tell your men to load the truck," Wentworth directed. "I am going to be right beside you. This gun will get you through the belly the instant you try to trick me."

A stream of lead poured into the body of the fiend who was about to lash Jenkyns!

Schwieder's under-sized eyes blazed with hell's fury, but he did as he was directed.

"They may get me, if you try to call for help," Wentworth reminded, as the unsuspecting thugs lugged crated tommy-guns, cases of ammunition and boxes of dynamite and TNT into the truck, "but not before I empty this gun into your cowardly guts!"

Schwieder made no attempt to test that threat. Meekly, he watched the loading completed and walked over to the truck, as ordered. He stepped to its left running-board and climbed up under the wheel when Wentworth's pocket-concealed gun prodded him.

"You're taking this ride—with me, Schwieder," Wentworth snapped. "Tell them you're going to show me the route out of town and will be back later. Then I'll tell you where to drive."

Sullenly, Schwieder stepped on the starter and threw the car into gear. Wentworth never lost the drop on the fuming killer at his side. It had been touch and go every second, but he had staked everything on his belief that Schwieder was yellow—and the desperate gamble had succeeded!

Like a cornered rat, Schwieder was eying him viciously, waiting for the first opportunity to spring at him and get the upper hand; but Wentworth never gave him that chance. As soon as they reached a dark road on the edge of town, he stopped the truck and made the killer get out. He forced Schwieder to take off his suit and then lie on the road. His wrists and ankles were tied with the same ropes that had held Wentworth so securely.

With the gangster piled in on top of the truck's cargo of death, Wentworth drove on to the first telephone he found. There he called the Warrenville police headquarters. He reported the location of the gang's headquarters—where the murdered corpse of Solly Klein would be sufficient evidence to hold them all in jail until their other crimes could be proved against them.

"Who are you?" the astonished desk sergeant was demanding. "How do I know you're on the level? Where—"

"This is a tip from the Spider!" came the curt reply, and Wentworth hung up before a police car could be rushed to that booth to apprehend him.

BACK AT the wheel of the truck, he drove as fast as he dared. As the miles slipped past, he debated what must be done with his dangerous cargo. Much as he hated to put these deadly weapons into the hands of the gangsters, it was imperative that he deliver them in order to gain Hilo Flynn's confidence. Once he knew the racketeers' plans, he would have to make a desperate bid to destroy the explosives before they could be used.

Before they could be used? But perhaps it would be possible to turn at least some of them against the gangsters themselves!

There was little time now to seek a hiding place, but Wentworth watched intently until he found a boarded-up store on the outskirts of Harper's Falls. Behind it was piled a stack of barrels and boxes. Quickly, he unloaded three of the tommy-guns and several cases of ammunition. These he buried in the pile with the desperate hope that no curious prowler would uncover them.

Next, he turned his attention to disposing of Pete Schwieder. He drove along the river road until he came to a spot, just above the town, where was beached an old scow. An excellent hiding place for the gangster until it proved convenient to hand him over to the law!

Schwieder's eyes were wild with terror, when he was hauled out of the truck. Broken pleas babbled from his lips, as he cowered away from the expected bullet or knife he would unhesitatingly have given Wentworth had their positions been reversed. A gag soon stifled his yammering, and Wentworth dragged him to the edge of the hulk, boosted him on board and dropped him into the empty hold.

Back at the truck, Wentworth set to work with his make-up kit and removed every trace of the frowzy face that was Blinky McQuade's. Expertly, his fingers worked. When finished, the face that looked back at him from the make-up mirror was hard and cold-eyed—that of a killer who would have received short shrift at the hands of any jury. Quickly, he changed into Schwieder's suit—and was ready to meet Hilo Flynn!

But before reporting at the gangster headquarters he had to know that Nita was safe.

It was after eight o'clock, but he made a circuitous entrance into the town in order to stop at the Warwick Hotel. Secure in his disguise, he walked up to the desk and asked for Miss Cameron. He was informed that she was no longer registered there.

"They checked out early this morning," the clerk told him. "No forwarding address. That's all I can tell you about them."

Nita had checked out—why? Where could she and the others have gone? Certainly, they would not have left Harper's Falls without him. She must have had to flee, been *driven* to another hideout. That was the answer! Tingling with apprehension, Wentworth regained the truck and drove to the mill. He parked in front of the gate, then went hunting Hilo Flynn.

Flynn came on the run. He glanced at the note from Schwieder and shook hands with "Lucky Lobin"—but it was the truck load of supplies that interested him most.

"Hell—I thought the stuff would never get here," he grumbled as he swung in behind the wheel and drove around to a parking-space where a dozen cars were lined up. "What's the matter with Pete? He knows I gotta have that soup for tomorrow morning." He cursed because there were not as many guns as he expected. Only the boxes of high explosives mollified him.

"That's the stuff!" He caressed the tightly sealed containers with his fingers. "We'll use some of the dynamite tonight, but we'll need all the other stuff tomorrow. You're just in time to join the party, Lobin." He grinned. "We're gonna teach this punk chamber of commerce how to keep their yaps shut. You can come in my car."

Flynn led him to a big sedan where three other gangsters were already waiting. The other machines were now filling up also. There must be nearly fifty of the thugs, Wentworth counted, as the cars got under way—fifty blood-thirsty killers to be turned loose on those courageous businessmen who dared refuse to pay tribute!

"They're having a mass meeting in the high school auditorium," Flynn told him. "All the biggest bellyachers. But when we get through with them they'll have something to holler about!"

An indignation meeting in the high school auditorium—that

meant women and children would be there. Hundreds of unsuspecting people were walking into a trap that would cave in on their heads when the building was dynamited. But it would not be dynamited, Wentworth resolved grimly, as his nails dug into the palms of his hands! Those innocent people must be saved no matter how he accomplished it.

A block from the high school, the cars drew up at the curb and the gangsters came to Flynn for final instructions. In groups of four and five, they started toward the building, carrying the packages of dynamite with which it was to be blown up.

Too late Wentworth realized that there was no way in which he could prevent the setting of those charges or save the building from destruction. Yet, somehow, he *must* save those unsuspecting victims! Somehow they must be warned!

WATCHING INTENTLY for a possible break, he suddenly noticed that he was almost alone. A stranger to the others, he had no definite part in this murder program—he almost occupied the role of a bystander as they went into action. Flynn was too busy giving orders to pay any attention to him—to notice that Wentworth stepped farther and farther back into the shadows, and then disappeared entirely....

Quickly, Wentworth ran to the school building and reconnoitered it. It was long and low, with a center unit and two wings. One, lighted, must be the auditorium. Coming closer, he saw the lighted doorway and a knot of earnestly talking people in the lobby. But if he tried to gain admittance through there, he would be shot down before reaching the door.

He went around to the rear of the building and found another entrance—a door at the head of a flight of steps. It was the stage door! This was a break!

Hastily, he padded up the steps and tried the door. It was locked, but he probed at the keyhole, with one after the other of a ring of skeleton keys. Finally, one worked. The lock clicked, and he stepped inside. He took a few steps and found himself backstage, looking out on the rostrum where a speaker was addressing the crowded hall.

Wentworth was on the verge of dashing out onto the stage and sounding the alarm, when he remembered his present appearance. Instead of heeding his warning, they would believe him a member of the gang, and throw him into jail. They would sit there and meet their doom. He must find some other way to shock them into a realization of their peril.

His desperate eyes saw the microphone in front of the speaker. It was the answer! If that amplifying system were only hooked up directly with the backstage control panel....

It was hooked up! Wentworth located the panel, stepped up beside the man who stood in front of it and jabbed a gun into his back. The fellow's head pivoted, eyes widened like saucers, lips started to open. Wentworth's flinty glare silenced him. Speechless, he backed against the wall, held his hands over his head. Wentworth grabbed the controls, cut out the speaker's microphone and plugged in the backstage connection.

"Sit still and listen to me!" His voice, harsh and rasping, boomed out into the hall, drowning the efforts of the surprised speaker. "Don't be alarmed—this is no time for panic. Get out of this hall as fast as you can. It will be dynamited at any moment!

This is no joke!" he snarled at them, as they kept their seats and several began to laugh nervously. "Get out, if you value your lives! This is the Spider!"

Now they understood. With screams of terror, the women got to their feet and started for the aisles. Calmer, some of the men took charge and prevented a panic as the auditorium emptied in record time, cheating those blood-thirsty devils of their prey.

Leaving the gaping-mouthed electrician standing beside the control panel, Wentworth ran to the stage door and out into the night just as the building trembled, ceiling crashed down and walls crumbled. Suddenly, the dynamite charges roared their destructive spite, but now they were too late! The "chief's" bloody coup had failed; the intended victims had been saved....

BUT WHEN Wentworth reached the front of the building wildest confusion confronted him. Women were screaming hysterically, men shouting and running for cover as shots rang out over the tumult. Mad panic reigned—but it was not because of the explosions and the crumbling building from which they had just escaped.

Hilo Flynn's killers were causing this new terror. Flailing about them with brutal automatics, they grabbed men and women, shoving them into automobiles which sped off down the street. They were the same cars which had brought the gangsters from the mill. Wentworth recognized them, as he ran up, gun in hand like the others, and dived into the one Flynn was just boarding.

Out of town and into the open country that cavalcade roared, to come to a stop at last beside a wooded grove—a grove which looked like the setting of a nightmare!

The savage killers were already venting their rage on the helpless victims who had rushed from the dynamited auditorium into their hands. Stripped to the waist, a dozen men dangled from trees by their bound wrists, devilishly suspended so that their toes just touched the ground. The flickering light of a dozen torches fell upon agonized faces, straining muscles—and the blank-faced thugs now flaying them mercilessly with long leather whips!

Those ashen-white faces were like death's-heads, corpse faces—and Wentworth understood why. White gauze masks covered the killers' entire faces and made them look ghastly.

The tortured victims screamed as they writhed under the pitiless whipping, their agony echoed by their wives who were compelled to stand by and look on.

Sick with revulsion, Wentworth glanced around the grove for some desperate chance. His eyes fell on Cliff Brackett. With a dozen of his fellow members, the chamber of commerce secretary lay on the ground, bound and helpless, awaiting his turn under the whips. Unlike most of the others, he was not palsied with fear. Veins stood out on his forehead, as he struggled with the ropes binding his wrists.

The ropes loosened. Now he had taken them off, was bending cautiously to unfasten his ankles. The ankle ropes fell away. Like a leaping tiger, he flung himself upon the killers, driving half a dozen of them from their moaning victims before he was overwhelmed and borne to the ground beneath a dozen punching, pounding thugs.

A splendid, madly heroic charge—but so pathetically hopeless!

Grim-lipped and helpless against such numbers, Wentworth watched those helpless humans undergo their cruel ordeal. Then he saw old Jenkyns dragged forward from a tree limb! Jenkyns would never be able to stand such punishment. He would die there under the whips.

That realization roused Richard Wentworth, at last.

DIVING BACK into the bushes, his expert fingers worked like lightning. Without the aid of a mirror, they yet performed a miracle of quick-change transformation. The straggly black wig, floppy black hat, long black cape—one after the other snapped into place. Now out of the brush leaped the snarling, maniacal-cackling figure of the Spider—just as the first whistling strokes of the lash fell on Jenkyns' back and the old man lost consciousness.

A stream of lead seemed to pour from the blazing guns of that ebon-hued nightmare. It cut down the thug who was lashing Jenkyns, then traveled around the vicious circle like a scythe of death. When the killers tried to return it, the darting figure was everywhere, nowhere. Seizing the lighted torches, hurling them into their faces, he loomed before them hideously… only to melt into the darkness before their bullets could find him.

"The Spider!" one of the panic-stricken thugs howled, and instantly the cry was echoed by a dozen others.

Even more effective than his deadly guns, that dread name

completed the rout Wentworth had begun. The gangsters broke and dashed wildly for their cars. The bolder of the quaking townsmen, quick to seize the Heaven-sent opportunity, rallied behind their weird champion and charged after them until the grove was cleared.

While the townsmen cut down their suffering fellows, Wentworth stooped swiftly over the fallen killers, to snatch up their guns—and to press the bottom of his silver cigarette lighter against the center of the forehead of each of those white masks.

Wherever it touched, the crimson replica of a spider crawled upon the dead victims—a warning to their fiendish master that the Spider was making good his promise!

Here was his answer!

Wentworth crept away....

Now his work began.

CHAPTER 9
HELL'S LOOM

WITH JENKYNS' unconscious body in his arms, Wentworth ran to one of the abandoned cars, propped the butler up in the seat and sprang behind the wheel. Anxiously, he scanned the old man's face. But as soon as the car got under way the cool air, blowing through the open windows, began to have its effect. Jenkyns stirred and his eyes blinked open.

"Tell me about it, Jenkyns," he demanded, his deft fingers removing the Spider make-up and restoring the face that was Lucky Lobin's. "Where is Miss van Sloan?"

Jenkyns tried to avoid those keen, probing eyes that had already detected and correctly interpreted his agitation. Bitterly, he recounted the story of the raid, of Nita's kidnaping and Ram Singh's death.

"Murdered," Wentworth repeated, a painful lump pushing its way up into his throat. "Left to be consumed by the flames like one of his noble ancestors on the funeral pyre… But there will be plenty to follow you to the hereafter, old friend!" he swore grimly. "They will atone for your death—from the lowliest killer to the inhuman devil responsible for it!"

First of all, he must find Nita. His steely fingers clamped crushingly around the wheel, as if the insensate metal was the throat of the criminal dog who had dared to lay a finger on her….

Wentworth's foot pressed down on the throttle, jammed it flush with the floor. But the car was old and could not keep pace with his raging frenzy. Twice another car passed him on the way back to town. The second one tugged at his memory, as it whizzed past at breakneck speed. It was a sleek tan convertible roadster very familiar… And then he placed it—Susan Conant's car!

But what was she doing on that road at such a time? Any one of a dozen innocent missions might have brought her there, reason reminded him. He dismissed all thought of her, as his mind sped back to Nita and the problem of locating her.

If the gangsters had Nita she probably was hidden somewhere in the shut-down mill buildings—and that was where he was going!

But who could be the master crook directing this malignant campaign against an unoffending and almost bankrupt town? Herbert Conant, George Atwood, Mayor Estabrook, Chief Skelly, or young Cliff Brackett? One by one, he considered the five who had sat in at the mayor's conference. One of them must have given the Judas tip that had inspired the rooming-house trap which almost cost his life.

Estabrook and Skelly seemed sincere, each in his own way. Atwood was too terrified for thought of anything except saving his own skin. Young Brackett had almost suffered a public flogging at the hands of the crooks tonight—might be dead or a captive in their hands at this very moment. Conant? The case against him was the most damning, and Wentworth resolved to have an interview with him in the near future. Meanwhile, Jenkyns could serve best at the Harper House.

"I want you to take rooms there for Miss van Sloan and yourself," Wentworth instructed. "Keep your eyes open for anything that appears suspicious. Watch George Atwood most closely of all. I will be back with Miss van Sloan as soon as I locate her."

That sounded very confident and matter-of-fact, but, when he dropped Jenkyns at the hotel and drove to the parking-space beside the mill building, Wentworth's nerves were taut with apprehension. Was she hidden away somewhere in that great, sprawling structure? Was she safe, or had those vicious thugs already....

STERNLY HE brushed such stabbing thoughts from his mind as he hailed the watchful guard and was allowed to enter. Down the corridor and into the big spinning-room, he went. The

SKELLY

KENDALL

ATWOOD

instant he strode in among the angry-faced gangsters, he sensed that something was wrong. The sudden hush which greeted him was significant. Flynn's suspicion was unmistakable.

"Hello, Lucky," he greeted with a tight-lipped grin. "Where you been all this time? We sorta missed you."

His mean, killer's eyes were glinting dangerously—those of a cat waiting for an unsuspecting mouse. Now the others were expectantly crowding closer, reaching surreptitiously for their guns. Wentworth realized that someone must have seen him donning the Spider disguise or had observed him making his getaway in the car—and recognized it as he drove it into the parking-space.

They had been waiting there, expecting him. But they were *not* expecting his sudden dive straight at Hilo Flynn—the split-second speed with which a pair of guns appeared in his hands. Before Flynn could spring his trap, Wentworth was upon him, knocking him out of the way, clubbing him to his knees— to crouch behind him and pour a withering blast of lead into the swarming killers.

Howls of agony echoed through the empty building. Before the snarling thugs could return his fire, the single electric bulb

SUSAN CONANT

CONANT

BRACKETT

dissolved into splinters and the spinning-room was plunged into darkness. Wentworth's pocket flash penciled ahead of him as he ran to the far end of the room and through an archway into the one beyond. Here his quick eyes spied a hand truck that offered the hiding place he needed. Crouching low behind its wooden side, guns ready for instant action, he heard the raging killers come pounding after him. Flynn was bellowing orders at them. "The doors—watch the doors! Some of you get outside and cover the windows! He can't escape! We'll find him!"

But they didn't find him. As soon as the room was quiet, Wentworth crept from his covert and padded softly into the corridor beyond. Room after room, corridor after corridor, he prowled through the dark, quiet mill. But nowhere was there any trace of Nita. Seemingly, the gangsters had been using only that one big spinning-room. He felt certain that she had not been there. Seemingly....

Suddenly, he tensed, ears straining to pick up a repetition of the sound he was sure he had heard. Long moments of heavy, blanketing silence followed—then he heard it again. It was a shrill scream, faint, far off—a woman's voice raised in terror or agony!

Like a lodestone, those screams drew him on. Louder and louder they grew, as he worked his way closer to the place from which they were emanating. Now there was no mistaking the throbbing agony that pulsed through them. They were the pain-wracked shrieks of a woman suffering beyond endurance!

Down into a basement he made his way, then to a sub-cellar beneath the level of the falls which supplied the mills with power. Past the dark turbine room… and now he was on the threshold of another cellar room that was like a chamber of the Inquisition!

Crowded around something in the center of that room were more than two dozen thugs—a slavering pack of bestial killers feasting their eyes upon a big machine spotlighted from overhead. They were filling their ears with the tormented shrieks that fairly made Wentworth's skin crawl. Sidling through the doorway, he worked his way into the room until he could see that machine—stare unbelievingly at the ghastly work it was performing!

ONCE AN innocent loom, Satan himself must have tampered with it—and produced a horrible contraption that never should have functioned outside of hell! It was studded with a row of long, wicked-looking needles that speared down into a flat metal bed. These needles were controlled by an eccentric drive which operated them in terrible, billowing waves that flowed up and down with tantalizing slowness!

On the metal bed beneath those blood-dripping spikes lay the body of a young woman. Her body was blood-soaked and writhed in agony. Two thugs, who presided over the machine, manipulated her so that the down-lancing needles speared through her flesh from head to foot, yet diabolically avoided the spots where their piercing thrusts would have meant the merciful reprieve of death.

Low moans came from her lips—almost drowned by the terrified shrieks of another bound girl who stood watching that horror with fear-maddened eyes. Wentworth glanced at her, and saw that there were *two* helpless girls held there in the hands of the thugs. The other, grim-faced, tight-lipped, was Nita van Sloan!

Savage-eyed, Hilo Flynn dominated that man-made hell. At his nod, the pain-wracked victim was thrust farther beneath those deadly needles. They champed up and down in her flesh, eating into her vitals, sewing a ghastly seam through her heart! With a final, agonized contortion, she went limp, freed at last by death. Now Flynn turned his evil eyes on Nita!

"Maybe you've decided to talk," he jeered, as his thugs stretched her out on the blood-wet metal bed. "Maybe you're gonna tell us where your boy-friend is. You better talk fast, sister—before those needles *sew* your mouth shut!"

A terrible rage surged through Wentworth, leaping hot and deadly from the very horror which overwhelmed him. It tensed him there ready to hurl himself upon those murdering devils. But he would have no chance against such odds—would merely throw his life away and doom Nita. He must take these rats by surprise, terrify them into momentary helplessness....

Swiftly, Wentworth recalled how the appearance of the Spider had disorganized them a short while ago. Again deft fingers went to work with a speed such as even they had never known. Frantic moments of feverish application, while Flynn baited Nita and tried to drag an answer from her tightly closed lips—and then the Spider's blood-curdling yell rang through the room.

His guns were out, ready to blast a way through the close-packed thugs as he leaped. But as his fingers constricted on the triggers, he was pounced upon. In a concerted rush they came at him, bearing him down, overwhelming him, tearing the blazing guns from his hands. Ropes snaked around his shoulders, legs, lashing him fast, tying him up in his black cape like a caterpillar in a cocoon.

Too late he realized that they had been expecting him. The way had been left purposely unguarded, so that he would step into the trap baited by the suffering girl's screams. Straight to that diabolical machine they bore him, dragging Nita to one side to make room on the metal bed.

"Remember," Flynn ordered gleefully, "he ain't to die too quickly. They tell me spiders have long lives. I wanta be shown. Give him plenty for every one of the men he murdered."

Desperately, Wentworth tried to press back, to draw his body away. Then they shoved him into the path of the needles. The first fearful spikes caught at the cloth of his cape. Again he was pushed farther. The sharp points were stitching through his coat, searing the flesh of his left arm like a succession of red-hot irons!

He heard Nita gasp, saw her slump to the floor in a faint at Hilo Flynn's feet. For that, at least, he was thankful as he steeled himself for the bite of those inexorable needles. Like hungry teeth, they chewed into his shoulder as the thugs twisted his struggling body. Cold sweat stood out on his face and he gritted his teeth. The next time he would be closer, the needles would go deeper—

But at that moment there came an interruption. His torturers hesitated, glanced at Flynn and turned startled eyes to the doorway. Now there was no mistaking the uproar that had caught their attention. Shots and yells, the pound of running feet—broke from somewhere upstairs!

Flynn cursed savagely and started for the doorway, gun in hand. He was swept aside, thrown back into the torture room, by the mob that came charging down into the sub-cellar. That mob that was led by Zella Gorman—composed of townspeople, armed with revolvers, rifles, clubs—any weapon they could find. Savagely, they tore into the gangsters, and the low-ceilinged room shook with the bedlam of roaring guns and bellowing voices!

"There's one of them!" Zella Gorman screamed above the din. "He's one of the skunks who killed my father!" Her blazing revolver bowled over a killer trying to find refuge behind the torture machine.

Like an Amazon, she battled her way across that powder-reeking room, cutting down the trapped gangsters and howling her men after any who managed to break through to the doorway. Cornered in their own trap, the gun-brave thugs paid dearly for the wanton killing of Jim Gorman....

REPRIEVED FROM the torture of those rotating needles, Wentworth inched himself carefully out of reach of their grasping points. Desperately, he wriggled and tugged at the ropes which held him fast, but made not the slightest headway—until a sharp knife started to slit through them, and Jackson's anxious face peered down into his!

"I got here as soon as I could, Major." Jackson was again the faithful sergeant reporting to the commanding officer who had become his idol on the battlefields of France. "They wouldn't come until they heard about that whipping tonight."

"Fine work, Jackson!" Wentworth commended, and the warmth of his grateful eyes was even more eloquent than his voice. "Never mind me, now," as Jackson freed his hands and arms. "Take care of Miss van Sloan."

Quickly, he tore the ropes from his legs and ankles, then knelt beside Nita, helping to untie her. Between them he and Jackson carried her upstairs and out of the building where she revived and was able to stand on her feet.

"Thank God!" she whispered, as they held her up. "Thank God—for you both! I didn't know what had happened to you."

"I tried my best to get away, but couldn't," Jackson panted an explanation and apology. "After I met Zella and her friends Saturday night, they would not let me go. I was practically a prisoner. It wasn't until tonight that they really trusted me."

"Tonight was all that mattered," Wentworth murmured thankfully. "Flynn's little whipping party certainly boomeranged and—"

He stopped short and drew Nita back into the shadows as the triumphant townsmen started streaming out of the mill. Now there was a new note in their noisy excitement, a new name on their lips. Flushed with their victory over the gangsters, they were intent on finishing the clean-up—streaming uptown, yelling and clamoring for Herbert Conant!

In their present mood, Wentworth could see, they would tear the banker limb from limb!

Swiftly, he stripped off the Spider's ebon habiliments and

obliterated every vestige of the ugly features so well known and feared by the high and the low of the underworld. That crowd of outraged townsmen had served him well, but they must not be allowed to degenerate into a mob. Even for men as heinously guilty as Conant appeared to be there were regularly constituted processes of law. Mob rule must not be allowed to flout that law.

"Jenkyns has a room waiting for you," he told Nita quietly when they reached the Harper House. "Jackson will stay with you."

"But, Dick—" an involuntary protest sprang to her lips.

"There are still things which must be done." His voice was low, persuasive, as he held her close. "It won't be long now, darling. I think the end is in sight."

With her kiss still warm on his lips, her fine courage stirring his heart, he hurried toward Herbert Conant's house in pursuit of the crowd. A block from the banker's home, he overtook them—just in time to see Susan Conant's sleek roadster speed into the grounds.

The crowd glimpsed that unmistakable car, too—and their threatening rumble swelled into a roar of rage. In a charging wave, they swarmed through the gate, over the fence, battling one another in their eagerness to lay hands on their intended victim. Shouting and yelling, they converged on the house— until Herbert Conant appeared on his porch and held up his hands appealingly.

"My friends, let me speak—" He tried to halt them, but they howled him down.

Missiles thudded against the porch, and the crowd surged in

to grab him—only to be hurled back by a blast of gunfire that poured into them from vantage points all over the grounds. It was a deadly blast from the pistols and tommy-guns of a score of hard-faced killers! Under that withering fire, the townsmen lost their eagerness. Dragging their fallen comrades with them, they fell back and dispersed when the gunmen charged and drove them back into the street.

This time there was no question about Conant's being under the killers' protection. And, as Wentworth took to his heels with the fleeing crowd, he determined to find out why!

CHAPTER 10
TERROR'S DEATH TRAP

FOR HOURS after the crowd had disintegrated, Richard Wentworth walked the streets of Harper's Falls. Devilment was in the air; he could sense it, his watchful eyes detecting its unmistakable signs. Usually, not a car was to be seen in the town after one in the morning. Tonight, he encountered almost a stream of cars with New York City license plates. Bands of men filled the usually deserted streets—men who gaped curiously and made jeering remarks about the hick town as they headed for its mill.

An army of crooks was converging on Harper's Falls, and a bloody dawn promised for the morning unless he—or Herbert Conant—could prevent it!

It was after three before Wentworth cautiously made his way into the Conant grounds. To his surprise he could detect no sign of guards around the place, even when he deliberately invited their attention by showing himself. Expecting every moment to be confronted by one of the killers, he crept up to the building.

The back door was locked and bolted, but his glass-cutter made short work of one of the lower windows. Reaching his arm through the small, round hole it carved in the pane, he turned the lock, lifted the sash and stepped inside—into darkness, utter silence. Like the grounds, there seemed to be no guards in the house. But as he padded softly from room to room he saw evidence of hasty packing.

Herbert Conant intended to flee—but would not before he had had a talk with Richard Wentworth!

Noiselessly, Wentworth went up the stairs to the second floor and chose the bedroom which seemed most likely to be Conant's. He opened the door. The pencil beam of his light flickered over the dresser, the bed—settled on the features of the sleeping banker.

Instantly, Wentworth was upon him, grasping his wrist, twisting it until his fingers relinquished the revolver they clutched desperately.

"You're going to talk, Conant," Wentworth said as he switched on the reading-lamp at the head of the bed. "Either you will do it readily or I'll beat the answers out of you with this. Yes—" as the banker's mouth sagged and his eyes widened—"I am Richard Wentworth. Now, tell me. Why are the thugs, who are terrorizing this town, so anxious to defend you?"

"I don't know," Conant quavered. "I swear to God I don't

know, Wentworth! I have had absolutely nothing to do with this awful trouble."

"How about that outfit you have quartered in one of the mills?"

Conant blanched, lips working nervously before he managed to force words from them. "Those are workmen—expert weavers," he said doggedly. "They came here expecting to find jobs in the reopened mills. If you doubt that, you can check it with Clifford Brackett—"

"Or perhaps with Clem Morley?"

That shot completed Conant's demoralization. Mortal fear leaped into his quailing eyes.

"So you won't talk about Clem Morley?" Wentworth's hand shot out, fastened in the banker's pajama collar and yanked him out of bed. "All right. If you won't talk to me, perhaps the crowd that came to visit you a few hours ago will be able to loosen your tongue."

"No! God, no!" Conant pleaded. "I'll talk—I'll tell you about Morley. Clem Morley lived here in Harper's Falls about thirty years ago. He got into trouble at the bank and was sent to prison for embezzlement. When he was sent away, he swore to be revenged against the town. Nothing more was heard of him after his term expired."

He panted. "We forgot all about him until this fearful scourge descended on the town. But since the outbreak of these crimes there have been threatening notes and telephone calls from him. He is here somewhere in the town—nobody knows where.

Either that—" Conant's eyes flickered almost imperceptibly—"or a clever crook is taking advantage of the legend."

"And you thought I was that crook," Wentworth nodded.

"It was a natural assumption," the banker admitted. "We knew nothing about you, and the trouble started shortly after your arrival. When we learned your identity it seemed to bear out my suspicions."

The man seemed sincere, and his answers had the ring of truth. Naturally enough, he was terrified. Wentworth attributed much of his peculiar behavior to panic more than anything else.

"I am taking your word—until I discover that you've lied to me," he decided. "But I don't want you to try to leave town. Your place is right here in Harper's Falls until this trouble is ended. If you try to leave, you will be stopped—the mob will tear you to pieces."

Conant gave his word not to attempt to escape and begged Wentworth to help him. His pleas were still ringing in Wentworth's ears, as he left the house to resume his tour of the town. **HOUR AFTER** hour, he walked, from one end of town to the other. By morning he had discovered that every road leading into Harper's Falls was closed with a detour sign. Ambushed behind each of the obstructions were hard-eyed killers to see that the orders were obeyed. Every telephone and telegraph wire had been severed, and communication with the outside world was virtually cut off. Overnight. Harper's Falls had become an imprisoned town—a private hell in the hands of an unknown devil free to work his will upon it!

Even the railroad depot was watched and patrolled by lynx-eyed killers. But the thugs made no attempt to interfere when the morning papers arrived. From them Wentworth learned that his coup in Warrenville had been a complete success. The entire gang was in jail and the hold of the racketeers on the town's business had been broken—thanks to the Spider.

Already, state officials, who had been contacted, were lauding the Warrenville police and urging other communities to do likewise. The criminal organization had been shaken—now it was up to Wentworth to shatter it here in Harper's Falls. But how? Where would he start?

With George Atwood, at the hotel—the answer flashed into his mind! Atwood, he remembered, had been on the verge of talking that morning at the mayor's conference. He was terrified, ready to crumble under the slightest pressure.

It was nearly ten o'clock before he was able to locate the Harper House proprietor. Finally, he managed to trick him into opening his door and cornered him in his private suite. One glance around the disordered room, and Wentworth surmised that, like Conant, the hotel man was preparing for flight.

"Take it easy, Atwood. You've nothing to be afraid of—from me," Wentworth assured him. "I'm here to save your life, not to injure you. But you've got to help me. I can't do a thing for you without cooperation. You've got to answer my questions, unless you want to go like Deckle and Henshaw."

Atwood caught at the back of a chair for support. Weakly, he sank into it and his tongue licked out over his dry lips. "I'll tell you anything you want to know."

"About Clem Morley?"

"I thought so," the hotel man nodded, and his eyes darted fearfully around the room. "Clem Morley used to live here in Harper's Falls," he took the plunge, and the story he told was substantially the same as Herbert Conant's—substantially the same, but not quite.

Morley, Atwood and Conant, he explained, had all been employed in the local bank, in the days of Morley's residence in the town. Morley was accused and convicted of embezzlement. It was not until after he had been sent to prison that Atwood discovered that Conant really was the guilty man. By then Conant had worked himself into such a position that it would have been very unwise to testify against him—so the matter was dropped.

"For a long time it was on my conscience," Atwood admitted. "But gradually, when we heard nothing more of Clem Morley, I forgot about it. Now he's back in town. He must have been watching us for years, waiting for the moment when he could step in and ruin us all just when we were going to put Harper's Falls back on the map."

So Herbert Conant really was the thief….And now Conant's bank would make thousands of dollars on the mortgaged properties which would revert to it because the owners had fled. More than that, his daughter Susan had been offering to buy out small businessmen who were only too anxious to sell at any price. Herbert Conant was once a thief, and now….

The telephone interrupted Wentworth's speculation. Atwood stared at it as if it would bite him. He reached for it with trembling fingers. As he listened, his pale cheeks faded to a sickly, fish-belly white.

Like one in a trance he put the receiver back on its hook.

"Clem Morley?" Wentworth prodded.

Atwood hardly seemed to hear.

"That was Sam Estabrook," he said dully, hardly seeming to realize that he was speaking. "The crooks have been holding him in his office for nearly twenty-four hours. They forced him to call on the state police for help. The troopers are coming this morning. But Sam said the thing was a trap—would be a slaughter. He started to say something about Clem Morley—and they must have shot him. I heard the report just before the receiver went down. Henshaw, Deckle—and now Sam Estabrook. He's killing us all, just the way he said he would!"

The state troopers were coming. That meant that they would arrive from their nearest barracks, forty miles to the east of Harper's Falls. Wentworth considered quickly. They would come by the east road into town—by way of the bridge crossing the river. Somewhere along that road a trap had been set for them— and suddenly he remembered the load of dynamite and TNT he had brought to town. Hilo Flynn had said he needed it this morning!

"He's going to kill us all!" Atwood's voice rose in a frenzy, and his eyes flamed with mad terror. "He called me this morning and told me my time to pay had come. I thought I could get away. But now it's too late! Morley—"

The name of his Nemesis was still on his lips when his voice strangled, was choked off in a wet, convulsive gurgle as he half-rose from his chair and toppled forward with a ghastly black hole drilled through his right temple!

The moment Wentworth heard the muffled crack of the silenced gun he flung himself to the floor. Then he was on his feet, one of his own weapons in hand, crouching and darting toward the half-open window. That window looked out on a shallow, railed balcony that ran along the front of the hotel. Instantly, he climbed out onto it, ran to the next window. This and the one beyond it were closed, the room behind them unoccupied and undisturbed.

Farther down the balcony... he was looking into the suite occupied by bedridden Willard Kendall and his physician. Kendall was trying to raise his bandaged head, muttering something unintelligible. But the moment the physician saw Wentworth he came running to the window.

"I saw him!" he called excitedly. "A man with a white mask over his whole face! He ran that way!" He pointed farther down the balcony.

The balcony was now empty. Undoubtedly, the fugitive had stepped through one of the windows farther along and by now had made his escape. Momentarily undecided, Wentworth hesitated—then his decision was made for him. Creeping along the road that girded the steep hill on the other side of the river, came the first of the state troopers' autos. Behind it came another, another—ten in all.

They were almost to Harper's Falls—speeding straight into the jaws of a death-trap!

CHAPTER 11
DYNAMITE!

A S WENTWORTH raced downstairs and dashed out of the hotel, he saw Susan Conant's tan convertible roadster in front of the door. But now there was but one thought in his mind—dynamite! In some way, he must prevent the slaughter he envisioned. He must stop those troopers before they reached the town!

Frantically, he sought for something, anything, he might use—and his eyes lit on a large truck. With desperate decision, he leaped on the running-board, grabbed the astounded driver and yanked him off the seat. Then, behind the wheel himself, he threw the roaring engine into gear. Straight for the bridge, he arrowed.

If only he could reach the other side before the troopers arrived! He might yet save them. If he could swing the truck across the road, it would block the bridge completely—*force* the troopers to stop and hear his warning. Out onto the bridge he thundered. He was going to make it—by a hair!

He was hardly past the center of the span when the whole world seemed to dissolve in a terrific, ear-splitting explosion! The floor of the bridge rose in the air crazily, iron girders twisted and snapped, the truck lurched at an impossible angle and started climbing to the clouds—then everything went down sickeningly, plummeting toward the river's surface!

The motor was still roaring furiously as Wentworth clung to the now useless wheel.

Below him the blue-green water looked as cold and hard as steel, a flinty surface against which he would be dashed to death. This was the end, he knew—yet, in that final brief moment, he was exultantly glad. He had sprung the trap, set off the explosives cached under the center of the bridge, and the troopers were cut off on the far side of the wrecked span.

Instinctively, his hands arched over his head and he hit the water in a dive—hit it with stunning force and went down, down into what seemed bottomless fathoms. Then he was back on the surface, bruised and dazed, paddling feebly.

Helplessly, the swift current bore him downstream, spun him around and around, buffeted him when he attempted to struggle against it.

But at that moment his water-bleared eyes glimpsed a battered canoe bearing down on him. A strangely familiar nasal voice shouted encouragement. Then he was being overhauled, held up by the collar, lifted aboard—to stare uncomprehendingly into the close-bearded face of Ram Singh!

AS IF a dream, Wentworth watched the Sikh bend over the paddle, heard the canoe swishing through the water, saw it dive into a black mouth that swallowed it, blotted out the light. Vaguely, he tried to understand.

Ram Singh was lifting him out of the canoe, helping him to stand, half-carrying him out from beneath a pier. Between a conglomeration of waterfront shacks the Sikh led the way until he turned in at an abandoned boathouse.

A bunk with a straw mattress was in the empty interior, and

Ram Singh stretched him out on it, massaging his wrists, gently kneading his forehead and the base of his skull.

"They thought I was dead when they left me in the store, but thy servant has many lives, master." He smiled. "I was nearly unconscious, but the flames awoke me to my danger. I crawled to the back and escaped through a window. There was nowhere else to go, so I came down here to the river where I had seen these empty buildings. This one sheltered me while I nursed my wounds and recovered my strength."

He nodded. "This morning the one true God must have guided my footsteps. I went up to the town to seek the *sahib* or the *missie sahib*, and it was given to me to witness the explosion that almost claimed the master's life.

"I go for water, master," he said quickly and seemed to vanish into thin air.

He had hardly gone before Wentworth heard his footsteps returning. He heard the footsteps at the back of the shed, the side, the other side beneath an almost opaque window, then at the door—heard them all over at once. But that could not be Ram Singh. There was more than one man out there—half a dozen, at least!

"Come out of there, Wentworth!" a gruff voice loudly commanded. "This is the police. You're surrounded—no sense trying to resist!"

They were all around the shack, several carloads of them. Wentworth saw them through a clean spot scraped on the begrimed pane.

"Come out before we start blowing the place to pieces!" the

THE SPIDER

He was hardly past the center of the span when everything

seemed to dissolve into a terrific explosion!

spokesman demanded. Wentworth gave up hope of flight. Groggily, he staggered to the door, opened it, and instantly was seized by two burly officers.

"Okay, Wentworth," the sergeant in charge growled. "I'm arresting you for the murder of George Atwood!"

"Atwood was shot down before my eyes," Wentworth protested as they dragged him to a car and thrust him inside. "I didn't kill him. He was murdered to shut his mouth—by the gangsters who have this town by the throat. They're making a fool of you," he tried desperately to convince the sergeant. "This charge is a frame-up to have me thrown into jail so that I can't interfere with their scheme to loot the town. Don't let them make a catspaw of you."

The sergeant was unimpressed. "That's *your* story," he grunted. "But we happen to have eyewitnesses who saw you put a bullet through Atwood without giving him half a chance. Your dirty game's about finished, Wentworth. Two of your crooks have squealed to save their own hides, and we know you're the big shot behind all this hell!"

EXHAUSTED THOUGH she was, after her ordeal in Hilo Flynn's torture room, there was little sleep for Nita van Sloan after she reached the Harper House and kissed Wentworth good-night.

Restlessly, she tossed, bitterly reproaching herself as the night hours passed. At last she dozed off to sleep—only to awaken the next morning and find that there had been no word from him. Now her sixth sense—an inner consciousness that in times of peril seemed to work in perfect rapport with his—whispered that he was in danger. He needed her!

A nervous tapping on the door interrupted this depressing chain of thought, and Nita sprang to answer it. In the hallway stood Susan Conant, trembling with excitement, her face white and scared.

"Mr. Wentworth sent me," she gasped, as soon as Nita had admitted her. "He—he was quite badly injured last night. We are hiding him so that those terrible gangsters can't locate him. He wants you, Miss van Sloan. He sent me to bring you."

"Mr. Wentworth sent you to bring me?" she hesitated doubtfully. "Then he must have given you a message—something that will convince me that he really is in trouble. Did he tell you anything?"

"No," the girl blurted impulsively. "That wasn't true, Miss van Sloan—he did not send me. But I knew that you would want to go to him. He keeps talking about you and calling for you in his delirium—"

Nita had heard, and now she knew why she had been so restless, had felt such persistent premonitions of evil. Delirium—meant Dick was badly injured!

Nita hurried down the stairs with her, followed her into the car as the girl glanced apprehensively up and down the street. Without interference, the roadster started away from the curb and sped across the town. But instead of heading for the mill district, as Nita had expected, it turned into the driveway of a large residence.

"This is my home," Susan Conant told her.

Richard Wentworth wounded and in hiding in Banker Conant's home? Nita remembered how Conant had led the police to the Henshaw estate, and her mystification and uneasiness increased. Curiously, she looked around her as they walked through the rooms of the lower floor. Dick was not there, but evidently in a bedroom on the upper floor. Susan Conant was leading the way to the stairs.

Nita was close beside her, followed her into a bedroom—and there the girl turned and faced her with mounting agitation.

"He isn't here, Miss van Sloan!" she almost sobbed. "Please forgive me for deceiving you. I had to do it—it was the only way I could get you to come with me. You *must* believe me!" she grasped Nita's hand and turned tear-dimmed eyes upon her. "I only tricked you into coming here to keep you out of jail. The police were coming to arrest you."

NITA WAS astounded, nonplussed by the girl's trickery and her mercurial changes. Susan Conant was an amazingly clever actress—and perhaps also a remarkably glib-tongued young criminal. Nita was uncertain about that.

"Probably, you meant well, Susan." She tried to appease the girl, "But I can't desert the others this way. I am going back to the Harper House to get Jackson and Jenkyns—"

At that moment the half-closed bedroom door was pushed wide, and tall, dignified Herbert Conant stood framed in the doorway. His eyes widened with surprise when he saw Nita.

"Why did you bring this young woman here, Susan?" he demanded sharply. "At a time like this! You should have known better—you know I want no strangers in the house."

Amazed by his ill-tempered, unmannerly outburst, Nita shook free of the girl's hands and started for the door. "I assure you I shall be no trouble to you, Mr. Conant," she shot at him icily.

"It's too late for that now," he said heavily. "Last night nobody could get into this house—and now nobody can get out. There are thugs guarding every entrance, and I was just told that their orders are to see that nobody leaves."

Utterly bewildered, Nita did not know whom to believe. Both the girl and her father seemed to be telling the truth—but both might be acting a part. Darting past them, she ran downstairs to the front door. But when she opened it two husky thugs barred her way in the vestibule.

CHAPTER 12
THE SPIDER CRAWLS

W HEN RICHARD WENTWORTH arrived at the Harper's Falls jail he found Chief Skelly waiting for him. Seated at the roll-top desk in his third-floor office, Skelly whirled around, his heavy-jowled face alight with grim satisfaction.

"Well, you come back to help us some more, have you, Wentworth?" he greeted as he waved to a chair beside his desk. "Any more questions you want answered—or maybe you know all about Clem Morley now?"

"I know what you're insinuating, Skelly," Wentworth said

129

patiently, "and that is just what the crook who is strangling this town wants you to think."

"Yeah, I know all about it," the police chief chimed in. "You never heard of Clem Morley, only—" he waved several sheets of typewritten paper in Wentworth's face—"I got two signed confessions here that tell just how you faked this Morley business in order to blackmail and rob the town. Best thing you can do is make a clean breast of it and help us clean up the rest of this scum you brought into town."

"Those confessions are fakes, Skelly," Wentworth said quietly.

"Don't worry your head about that." Skelly's face darkened angrily. "We'll take care of the town—"

"The way you took care of the mayor!" Wentworth flung at him. "He was murdered less than an hour ago—and the killers are holding his office at this very moment!"

"Sounds like you been hittin' the pipe, young feller," the old man jeered. "Mayor Estabrook happens to be out of town—gone to see the governor about this business. I was talkin' to his secretary not more'n ten minutes ago."

"And that was what the secretary was forced to tell you." Wentworth strove desperately to make him understand what was going on. "They probably were holding a gun up to his head while he talked to you. Don't you understand, Skelly. You're up against an *army* of criminals! Don't you see that they already have this town cut off from the rest of the world? They're going to blow it wide open! They're tricking you—"

"Maybe *you* thought you was trickin' me," Skelly snarled angrily. "But I had no use for you from the start. You thought you was pretty damn smart, but I knew you'd slip up some-where. You sure took a header when you let Cliff Brackett see you murder poor George Atwood."

"Brackett!" The name popped from Wentworth's surprised lips.

"Cliff Brackett swore out the murder warrant against you," the chief rasped, "and that's plenty good enough for me. You better let me know when you're ready to talk, Wentworth."

Still puzzling over that astonishing development, Wentworth was led away—to a fifth-floor cell from which he could look out over the street and hear the uproar that was arising from it.

The building was being besieged! Driven back into their own headquarters, the penned-up police were desperately return-ing the fire, matching their revolvers against the lead-spouting tommy-guns that hosed death through every window where a head appeared.

WENTWORTH'S JAWS clenched grimly. He silently cursed Joe Skelly's stubborn-headed stupidity as he real-ized what that siege meant—a city of twenty thousand souls, deprived of its police protection, was now entirely at the mercy of the blood-thirsty criminal horde overrunning it!

At the mercy of a ruthless butcher who laughed contemptu-ously as he turned loose his vicious destroyers!

Suddenly, the arch-criminal's jeering voice began to taunt him; seemed to shout right into his brain—a demoniacal over-tone to the tumult below. It seemed to be right at his ear, and when Wentworth backed away from the cell window he under-stood. In one of the cells down the corridor a prisoner had a radio. He was dialing along the short-wave band when a penetrating voice came in clear and loud.

"For those who have not heard, I repeat." It mouthed each word with evil relish. Wentworth knew that he was hearing the voice of the almost mythical Clem Morley!

"This is my homecoming, my repayment to the town that railroaded me to prison and left me to rot there!" it chuckled derisively. "Harper's Falls forgot all about Clem Morley and the indignities he had suffered. But Clem Morley did *not* forget. Clem Morley set down on his bill every day of unjust confinement, every hour of humiliation and heartache. Now Harper's Falls is going to foot that bill!"

He went on. "Harper's Falls wronged and persecuted me, but now it is going to serve me. It will serve as an example and warning to any other towns that may be so foolish as to think that they can succeed in opposing the organizers of the Cooperative League. Watch what happens here this morning—then remember that the fate of Harper's Falls will be meted out to any other town that dares to defy my organization!"

Wentworth listened to no more. There was no doubting the sincerity of those mad threats. This criminal monster could, and would do just what he said. Even Joe Skelly must now realize it. Loudly, Wentworth shouted for the guard.

"I want to see Skelly," Wentworth demanded. "Tell him—tell him that I'm ready to talk."

In a few minutes the guard was back, and Wentworth was led down to Skelly's office.

"YOU HEARD that broadcast," Wentworth nodded to the

office radio that was still popping after the raucous voice had finished. "Surely you must realize what you are up against, Skelly. You are helpless here in your own headquarters."

But the bull-necked chief was unimpressed.

"Yeah, I heard it," he grunted. "I s'pose you think it was a pretty slick trick to make me think that the man I want is still at liberty. But I'm not fallin' for it—not today. I'll take my chances on that gang of yours. So long as I have you locked up here in jail, there's not much fear they'll try to dynamite us."

The man was blind, absolutely impenetrable in his own self-sufficiency.

Now Wentworth took the only alternative. "You win, Skelly." He shrugged his shoulders, resignedly. "I'll sing, if you give me a break."

"It'll go easier for you, if you come clean," Skelly agreed eagerly.

Wentworth nodded glumly, and the chief sent the waiting guard for a stenographer, cleared a place for them at the pamphlet-littered table in the center of the office. The stenographer was a husky young cop of about his own age—which made the odds three to one against him.

"My real name is Richard Wentworth, although I came to Harper's Falls under an alias," he began dictating, sparring desperately for time. "Under the name of John Stafford, I rented the Nathan Henshaw estate and set up my headquarters there. I picked Harper's Falls because I knew the town was on the verge of a business boom, and because I had once contacted an ex-convict named Clem Morley and learned his story—"

"So you know Morley, eh?" Skelly interrupted with quick interest, as he came over to the table and stood behind the stenographer. "When was that?"

"About a year ago," Wentworth answered. "He was bitter against the town and gave me the low-down on the whole crowd of you—Henshaw, Atwood, Conant, Estabrook, Deckle and you, Skelly—"

"I didn't have any hand in sending him away," the old chief defended himself quickly. "I was just a young cop then. I had to pick him up, but that wasn't—"

In his eagerness to clean his hands of any responsibility for what had happened to Clem Morley, he leaned over the stenographer's shoulder—and unwittingly placed himself between Wentworth and the jail guard who still stood near the office door.

Wentworth's alert eyes were quick to see that—just as they had noted the revolver which Skelly had left lying on his desk. Restlessly, he wriggled on his chair, stretched his long legs farther under the table—then suddenly leaped to his feet like the released spring of a trap, to upend the heavy table full in the stenographer's lap!

Borne over backwards by the sudden upheaval, the policeman teetered on his chair and crashed into Skelly's middle, just as Wentworth came diving in a flying leap. His fist smashed up under Skelly's out-thrust chin with all the perfectly coördinated strength of his lithe, athlete's body. Then he was at the desk, snatching up the chief's revolver, to bring it down over the slow-thinking guard's head before he had a chance to more than half-draw his own weapon.

Revolver in hand, Wentworth stood over the stenographer, as he dazedly staggered to his feet and gaped, open-mouthed, at the still bodies of Skelly and the guard.

"Off with your uniform!" Wentworth snapped, as he relieved the stenographer of his revolver. "Put it there on that chair. Now lie down on the floor and put your hands behind you."

Meekly, the policeman obeyed. Without a sound, he lay flat while Wentworth handcuffed him with his own manacles, gagged him with his own torn shirt, then lashed his ankles to a leg of the overturned table with his belt. Quickly, Wentworth stripped off his suit, put on the uniform, catfooted to the door and opened it warily.

THE CORRIDOR was empty. Evidently, no attention had been attracted by the brief struggle—but Wentworth realized that he had no time to lose.

There was an unbarred window at the end of that corridor. Wentworth walked to it with pretended unconcern, looked out—then his heart leaped! Below the window, next door to the jail, was the flat roof of a one-story garage!

Quickly, he lifted the sash to its full height and looked out. Gangsters were opposite the garage, covering the lower floors of the combination police headquarters and jail with their fire. No bullets, however, were coming as high as the third floor. If he moved swiftly, he should be able to make it before being spotted....

Wentworth's fingers unfastened the uniform tunic, unwinding the long, slender silken rope that was wrapped loosely around his body. Tying one end to the foot of a corridor radiator, he dropped the rest out of the window. Then he climbed onto the sill, left it and went down the tough silken strand, hand over hand. The Spider darting to safety on a tenuous thread of his web!

Bullets came seeking him before he was more than halfway to the garage roof. But he shoved himself away from the building wall, swung like a pendulum until sufficiently low to release the rope—then dropped the rest of the way. Yells from the street told him that the gangsters understood his intention and were running to the garage to head him off. Before they could reach it, he had leaped from the roof to the back yard, dashing inside, threatening guns held ready. He flung himself behind the wheel of a heavy coupé now having its motor tuned.

"Open that door!" he shouted.

They quickly sprang to obey—and then he was rolling out into the street, jamming his foot down on the throttle, bending low over the wheel as he sped through a hail of bullets.

Already, he was formulating a plan—but first he must run that fiery gauntlet.

Bullets spattered against the car, drilled and starred the windshield, *spanged* against the doors.

Ahead of him, on the edge of town, loomed a detour barricade—a wooden horse reinforced with barrels at each end. Wentworth gripped the wheel, gave the engine every drop of gas it would take—and crashed through the obstruction. Splintered wood slapped against the shattered windshield, lead dinned against the metal top. But the car staggered clear, kept on its way to the boarded-up store where he had cached the tommy-guns and ammunition originally intended for Hilo Flynn.

Quickly, Wentworth recovered the hidden weapons, stowing them in the back of the bullet-battered coupé. Yet he knew that he could not hope to reenter the town in that car. So far, by a miracle, it had escaped. But such luck could not last—on the return trip it would be shot to pieces. The Daimler was the answer!

Wentworth stepped on the gas. Straight for the tumbled-down farmhouse, he headed. But, when he drove in beside it and got out, his vigilant eyes told him that someone had been here—the lock was off the barn door! That someone might be here still—waiting for him to return for the Daimler!

Warily, Wentworth started forward—just as the door swung open and Ram Singh stood smiling on the runway!

"I knew that the foolish police would not be able to hold the *sahib* overlong," the Sikh said gravely. "I knew also that the master would have need of the Daimler when he returned."

"Excellent, thoughtful one." Wentworth grinned his appreciation. "But besides the Daimler I need a supply of gasoline and the services of an expert auto mechanic."

"Both can be secured at one time, master," Ram Singh nodded as he took his place at the wheel of the limousine. "There is a gasoline station not far from here whose proprietor feels that he owes thy servant a debt of gratitude."

Phil Bunce remembered that debt. The moment he recognized the Daimler, he came running up to shake the hand of the man who had saved him from a beating that probably would have meant his death.

"*Will* I jump at a chance to get a crack at those dirty rats!" Bunce whooped the moment he understood the part he could play. "I'm not much good at fist-fighting—but you couldn't keep me out of this!"

He quickly gathered a kit of tools while his assistant filled several five-gallon cans with gasoline and stowed them in the limousine.

"A can of red paint and a brush, too, if you have them," Wentworth added as an after-thought.

Then the Daimler was headed back to Harper's Falls—for the rebuilt detour barricade which promptly scattered in every direction under its smashing onslaught.

Back through the deserted streets to the front of the half-demolished high school, Ram Singh drove. On the lawn in front of the building stood a camouflaged tank—a World War souvenir that Wentworth had remembered having seen rumbling along the streets of Harper's Falls in a parade.

That memory had been his inspiration....

WHILE RAM SINGH went to work with an acetylene torch on the heavy chain which anchored the tank to its concrete foundation, and Bunce busied himself with the motor, Wentworth began wielding the paint-brush. On the steel top and sides he daubed the brilliant red paint. When he was finished three large crimson spiders sprawled over the discolored camouflage!

"The Spider would appreciate this," he chuckled grimly for

the filling station man's benefit. "But as long as he can't be here, all three of us will carry on for him."

Ponderously, the tank rolled off the lawn and clanked its way over the sidewalk and into the road. Slowly, it rumbled to the center of town—and when it nosed its way into the gangster-held area two tommy-guns were pouring a leaden blast from its revolving ports.

With yells of terror the gangsters took to their heels as that destroying monster bore down upon them. But it pursued them relentlessly. Up and down the battle-scarred street, it ranged—a grim old veteran returned to the wars, to serve its country once more against a slinking, cowardly enemy far more insidiously dangerous than any who ever had the courage to don a uniform.

Its blazing guns were too much for those cravens who had been so brave in bullying helpless, unarmed, law-abiding citizens. Even more effective in striking terror to their yellow hearts was the blood-chilling insignia of their Nemesis, the Spider!

In headlong panic they fled, many to be pounced upon and dragged down by the infuriated townsmen who followed in the wake of their steel-clad liberator. Then the police, the siege of their headquarters lifted, swarmed out to join the fray—and the gangsters' rout was complete.

The killers were scattered, their reign of terror momentarily ended. But there could be no peace for Harper's Falls until their infamous master was uncovered and made to pay for every drop of blood he had spilled, for every bit of needless misery caused….

Richard Wentworth's work was not yet done—and now he

THE SPIDER

could take no chances of having anyone stop him. Chief Skelly's powers of perception were so notably deficient that even now he might not understand. Wentworth would take no chance of being thrown back into a cell. Twisting the wheel sharply, he sent the tank careening up onto the sidewalk—crashing through the front of a looted jewelry store.

"Stay here and cover me," he called to Jackson, as he climbed out and dived behind an overturned counter.

Screened by the tumbled wreckage, he made his way to the back of the store, to where a door led out to a delivery alley. The alley was deserted. And just as the police came in to help their rescuers from the tank, Richard Wentworth slipped out through the rear—finally, to settle with Clem Morley!

CHAPTER 13
SHACKLES SHATTERED!

THE HARPER HOUSE looked deserted when Wentworth strode through its front door. Most of the guests were mingling with the wide-eyed crowd hovering on the edge of the Main Street battleground. But the guest Wentworth had come to see would not be with them. That guest would be right there in his room, waiting....

Straight to the suite occupied by Willard Kendall, financier, Wentworth went. Cautiously, he grasped the knob and, as he expected, found the door locked. Crouching beside it, ears strained to catch the slightest sound from within, he noiselessly plied his skeleton keys on the old-fashioned lock. The second one sprang the bolt. Gun in hand, he stepped inside.

The bed-ridden man was alone—but he popped up to a sitting position with remarkable agility when he glimpsed his visitor. Eyes, wide with fear, stared out of the swathing bandages. His lips opened to shout an alarm. But before a sound could come from them, Wentworth leaped upon him, forced him back onto the pillow—and relentlessly ripped away the yards of gauze that concealed nearly all of his face.

Off came those mummy bindings—to reveal the face of a man totally unhurt! It was the face of a man who looked a great deal like Willard Kendall but was *not* the New York financier!

"A fake, eh?" Wentworth flung at the terror-stricken wretch.

As he had figured, the man was an impostor—a dummy playing the part of a blind. The attack on this man had been deliberately staged so as to confine him, the *supposed* Willard Kendall, to his room—while the *real* Kendall was at large!

"You got away with it beautifully for a while, but the game is up." Wentworth's voice was knife-edged, brittle. "This town is mighty anxious to locate Clem Morley. When I tell them that I've found you—you'll be lucky if the police get you to jail alive."

"Morley? My name ain't Morley! I never heard of nobody named Morley!" the fellow babbled.

"If you're not Morley, why are you lying here pretending to be Willard Kendall?" Wentworth's demand cut short his tirade. "Who arranged this fake—who put you up to it?"

Relief flashed momentarily in the impostor's eyes, and

Wentworth saw that the fellow was getting onto more familiar ground—now about to lie.

"I oughtn't say nothing," he whined, pretending to glance around the room apprehensively. "This is gonna put me on a spot, if he finds out I squealed. But I ain't taking no chances with my neck for Herb Conant—"

The banker's name had hardly left his lips, when a board creaked. Kendall's supposed physician loomed there in the side doorway. Instinctively, Wentworth ducked—just as a bullet from a silenced automatic buried itself in the fake financier's brain.

Jack-knifing himself from the floor, Wentworth was after the killer before the muffled echo had stilled. He flung himself through an open window of the adjoining room, leaped out onto the narrow balcony—just in time to snap a shot at the fugitive climbing into another room. That bullet sped true—and in bringing down the murderer it settled the score for George Atwood as well.

But this killer was only a minor cog in the crime wheel. The man responsible for him was still at large. Wentworth was almost certain that he was not Herbert Conant—equally confident that he knew where the cunning scoundrel could be found.

The Henshaw estate! Empty since he had left it, and now tied up by the death of Nathan Henshaw—what better hiding place for one who wished to be free from all interruption or interference?

WENTWORTH FOUND a cab that took him within a block of the Henshaw place and went the rest of the way on foot. As he crouched in the bushes near the drive, he realized that his suspicion was correct—one by one the routed gangsters were converging on the estate. Carefully, he avoided them, worked his way up to the house.

The building was quiet and seemingly, deserted. It gave no indication of the presence of the desperate killers whom he was positive it sheltered. To try to gain admittance by way of the doors would be foolhardy, suicidal. But Wentworth knew this house well. Creeping close to it, sheltered by a high growth of lilacs, he darted through a side opening beneath the front porch. Then he crawled to a cellar window that opened when he thumped against it with the heel of his hand.

Now he could hear the low rumble of voices upstairs in the front rooms. There was a flight of stairs at the rear which led to the kitchen and pantries. Wentworth reached them safely, started along the short corridor leading to the front—and abruptly flattened against a nook in the wall as a figure loomed ahead of him. It was a gray-haired man with a ghastly white face!

This man turned into a room that Nathan Henshaw had used for a library and office. Before he could close the door behind him, Wentworth reached him, jabbed a gun into his ribs and thrust him inside. Spinning the fellow around, Wentworth saw the reason for that colorless countenance. It was a white gauze mask such as the whippers at the grove had worn.

"What are you trying to hide, Kendall—your own face or Clem Morley's?" Wentworth snapped. "I know they're the same face!"

They had to be the same face. Kendall *had* to be Morley—it was the only logical explanation for that masquerader back in the Harper House bed. This man was the *real* Willard Kendall. He had come to Harper's Falls, but realized that, in his old home town, he would be recognized as Clem Morley. For this reason, he had arranged the substitution that would keep his secret safe and also allow him to indulge the murderous revenge he craved.

Wentworth's hand darted out, gripped the side of the mask. He tore it from the bleak, rage-blanched features of the financier he had so often seen in New York.

"So the Kendall part of my guess is correct," Wentworth said, backing the old man toward the door. "When I get you down to Chief Skelly we'll find out soon enough whether you are Clem Morley. He'll recognize Morley all right."

Tight-lipped, murderous-eyed, Kendall said not a word as he was forced toward the corridor's rear entrance that would start him on his way to the electric chair. Wentworth gripped the door, started to open it—and was almost knocked off his feet as it slammed inward under the charge of a half a dozen thugs!

Before he could fire, someone leaped on his back, another gripped his gun-wrist and twisted it powerfully. He saw that others had swarmed in from a side door and window. Quickly, they disarmed him, hemmed him in. A dozen of Kendall's killers—led by Cliff Brackett!

"THAT WAS very well timed, Cliff," Kendall commended. Then he turned to Wentworth, his eyes narrowed to blazing slits, his face twitching as if he were suffering with St. Vitus's dance. "Yes, Mr. Wentworth," he said, his voice a mocking purr, "I am the one this town once knew as Clem Morley—as you so cleverly deduced. I admit I did not intend that to become known. But there is very little chance that it will."

He explained. "When I came here and found you so conveniently located in the town, the opportunity was too good to be missed. I decided to have you blamed for what would occur—or, rather, to have you share the blame with Herbert Conant. For Conant is the one who must pay most dearly for the wrong he inflicted on me!"

At the mention of that old wound. Kendall's face fairly convulsed.

"I held the bag for Conant's thievery! I went to prison for him!" he raged. "But now he is paying! I have made it appear that *he* is responsible for bringing my men to town, that *he* is benefiting by their activities, that *he* is working with them and using the old Clem Morley episode as an excuse to rob and pillage the town! It has taken time and work, my dear Wentworth—but labor such as this is sweet."

He went on. "Conant was well entrenched here—the big man of Harper's Falls. He had to be undermined carefully. For that reason, I sent Cliff Brackett here a year ago. For that reason, he paid court to Herb Conant's daughter and gradually wormed his way into Herb's confidence. He was successful in interesting Willard Kendall in the plan for rejuvenating this worthless, has-been town. Careful, painstaking work—but it succeeded! Herb Conant is a discredited, ruined man—half-mad with fear. He's a trapped rat who doesn't know where to turn!"

Kendall chuckled with demoniacal enjoyment. "He's paying—he and his brat. And that Miss van Sloan of yours, as

145

well, Wentworth. They are paying right now. They are all penned up in Conant's fine big house. But the guards which I furnished him last night have departed—all except a few who are there to see that nobody *leaves* the house, instead of keeping intruders away. The mob that tried to break into the place last night is reorganizing—some of my men are seeing to that. By now they should be storming the house and howling for Conant's blood—worked up to such a pitch that they will drag their victims out and tear them to pieces or string them up to the nearest tree!"

Clifford Brackett had flushed when Kendall revealed his duplicity, had avoided Wentworth's eyes. Uncomfortably, he had listened to the old man's fuming tirade. Now he was ashen-faced.

"I didn't know that Susan was to be left there unprotected!" he protested anxiously. "You promised me that she would not be harmed—she and the van Sloan girl. But you've double-crossed me! You tricked me into getting them there in the house for you! I don't care what you do to Conant, but you're leaving Susan out of it. I'm going down there now."

Kendall held up a hand, checking Brackett as he tried to reach the door.

"You're getting soft, Cliff!" he jeered. "Falling in love like a sixteen-year-old! The girl will die with her father." The mocking laughter suddenly wiped out of his eyes and his voice was steely, barbed. "I'm only sorry there aren't more of them to pay!"

Brackett's glance flashed from one to the other of the faces that surrounded him. He looked for sympathy, encouragement, a way out—but there was no compassion in those hard, brutal countenances.

"I have been doing your dirty work for five years, Kendall," he said bitterly. "I've been at your mercy ever since I was fool enough to play the ponies with money out of one of your cash registers. I would have paid that back, but you never gave me a chance. You jumped on me and held the shortage over my head like a club."

"It seems to me there was the Little matter of a murder mixed up with that unfortunate shortage," Kendall reminded softly.

"That was a frame-up—you know it as well as I do!" Brackett flared. "I had nothing to do with that killing. I can prove it. I could clear myself, if you'd give me the chance—but you won't. You've used the murder charge to shackle me. That was the only reason I came up here to Harper's Falls and made a louse of myself by playing your dirty game. You forced me to win Conant's confidence and then trick him into bringing your killers into town, in the belief that they were the weavers you insisted on having here before you would reopen the mills. You forced me to play up to Susan and trick her into doing things that would rebound against her and her father."

Brackett's face was working under the stress of his emotion.

"You forced me to be a dirty cad," he excoriated himself. "But you couldn't stop me from falling in love with her. You saw that, so you let me believe that, in the end, I would be able to save her and take her away with me. And now you think you're going to—"

SOMETHING SNAPPED then. Driven to utter desperation, young Brackett threw discretion to the winds and flung himself at his grinning tormentor—which was just what Wentworth had seen coming. Almost simultaneously, he dived low and charged, head-on, into the belly of one of the thugs. He caught the fellow, as he doubled up, and hurled him into the midst of his fellows. Like an agile boxer in a battle royal, Wentworth leaped around that room, seeming to face all directions at once, as his fists pistoned into snarling faces and soft, flinching stomachs.

The berserk fury of his attack swept them off their feet, gave them no chance to take the offensive. When they did manage to draw their guns, he was crouched low behind Willard Kendall, holding the quaking financier in front of him for a shield.

"Don't shoot!" Kendall screamed at his men in wild terror, as he felt the cold muzzle of an automatic boring into the back of his neck. It was the automatic he had been trying to tug from his pocket when Wentworth wrested it from his fingers. "You'll hit *me!* Come in and grab him!"

"If they do, you will never know it," Wentworth said calmly at his ear. "The first hand that touches me will pull this trigger."

Kendall heard the safety catch click off.

"No—no!" he howled, trembling arms held out in front of him, fingers widespread, as if to push them back. "Don't come any closer! Stay back! He'll do it—he'll kill me!"

"Throw down your guns—on the floor there in the center of the room," Wentworth commanded.

They started to snarl obscene refusal. But Kendall raged at them, commanded them to obey. Sullenly, they complied. One after the other, their guns thudded onto the rug, where Bracket scooped them up and stuffed them inside his belt.

"Now, we're leaving," Wentworth announced, as he started his prisoners to the door. "There probably are other guns around this house, but remember—you can't kill me quickly enough to save Kendall's life. If you get me, he goes, too."

Kendall was still warning them not to interfere, as Wentworth backed him down the corridor and out the rear door. Now was the crucial moment. No longer able to keep them in sight, Wentworth had no way of knowing whether those killers were scurrying for other guns.

Cliff Brackett raced to the nearest car, parked beside the garage. He sprang into the seat, whirred the starter. Warily, Wentworth backed away from the house, watching every window, every side. Then Kendall suddenly crumpled and slumped to the ground.

"Now!" Kendall shouted wildly, as he prostrated himself.

But Wentworth was over him in a flash, yanking him to his feet, rushing him into the approaching car. But it was too late. A shot roared from a clump of bushes and the bullet smashed through the financier's face! His last trick had boomeranged—bringing him death from the gun of one of his own killers, just arrived at the house!

WENTWORTH TRIGGERED a shot into the shrubbery, brought a howl of pain—another that bored through the skull of the killer as he leaped into sight. Those two shots were echoed by a dozen now blazing from the windows of the house.

Their lead thudded into Kendall's corpse and lanced fire through Wentworth's shoulder, as he heaved the body into the car and flung himself into the seat beside Brackett. Like a rocket, the car sped down the driveway.

Straight to police headquarters, Brackett raced. Chief Skelly was outside the building, viewing the damage that had been done to it—but all thought of that was forgotten the moment he caught sight of Wentworth.

"Never mind that now." Wentworth waved the gun aside. "You were so interested in Clem Morley a while ago—here he is!" He propped up the dead body of Willard Kendall.

"Damnation!" Skelly marveled. "That's Clem, all right. But how in hell—"

Cliff Brackett answered his amazed question before it was fully voiced. Swiftly, he narrated what had happened at the Henshaw house—and spared himself none in the telling. Frankly, he confessed his own part in furthering Kendall's diabolical vengeance scheme.

"I'm willing to take what is coming to me for that, Skelly," he finished, "but first you've got to rescue those girls! The mob may have them already. You will need every man you have—and *right away!* There isn't time—"

At last, Skelly seemed impressed. He shouted swift orders to his men, started to organize a rescue party. Yet, even now, he was the suspicious, bull-headed slow-thinker Wentworth knew so well.

"We'll take care of the girls, all right," Skelly rumbled as he gripped Brackett's shoulder, "but I'm holdin' onto you. You're stayin' right here where I know I can—"

Anticipating something of this sort, Wentworth had stepped

150

to the side of the car and slipped behind the wheel, hand ready on the clutch. Already, there had been too much talk, too much time wasted. He would wait for no more. Throwing the car into gear, he stepped on the gas and leaped away from the curb just as Brackett shook loose from Skelly's grip and sprang onto the running-board.

Blocks away from the Conant home, Wentworth could see the mob milling around in front of it, hear the savage roar that rumbled up from nearly a thousand people clamoring for the life of the man who had betrayed them. At the corner, he stopped the car, leaped out. The mob leaders had already broken into the house. They were dragging Nita and Susan Conant out onto the porch, to the steps, where the throng greeted them with a howl of wolfish delight!

"Daddy!" Susan screamed wildly as she struggled to tear loose from two huskies who half-carried her between them.

"God Almighty!" Cliff Brackett almost sobbed. "We're too late!"

Then he was clawing his way through the crowd like a madman, battling desperately beside Wentworth as they drove toward the porch in a spear-head.

Almost up to the porch now—and then Susan's terrified screams must have reached her father's ears. A French window opened on a second-floor balcony, and Herbert Conant stepped out. Ashen-faced, he looked down into that sea of snarling faces, heard the wave of abuse that stormed up at him. Then he spotted Richard Wentworth.

"There's your man!" he shouted above the roar of the crowd.

151

"There's the man you want—Richard Wentworth, a New York racketeer and murderer! He brought his criminal pack here and loosed them on you! He framed me—made you all turn against me because I would not sell out to him! Last night, he came here and threatened me!"

Conant was staking everything on a desperate gamble, going to any extreme in his frantic effort to turn that raging crowd. It looked as if he might succeed. The bedlam was quieting. Those within hearing of his strong, persuasive voice were listening. Then they heard another voice cry him down!

"No—no!" Susan Conant screamed. "That isn't true, Daddy— you know it isn't true! You've been hiding things too long! Tell them the truth—oh, *please*, Daddy!"

Like a graven image, Conant stood there on the balcony, lips half-parted, an orator stricken in the middle of his speech. His haggard eyes stared down at his daughter's pleading face. Wentworth could see the battle that was being fought behind them. But the pompous banker that Harper's Falls had once known was now crumbling, losing out....

"Susan is right—I have been hiding things too long." The Herbert Conant who had won at last looked down humbly, contritely, upon his neighbors. "It is because I hid things thirty years ago that all this trouble has come to our town. Yes—I hid the fact that I was a thief, and let Clem Morley go to prison for my crime. When Clem Morley came back to Harper's Falls with his army of thugs, I still tried to hide things so that my guilt would not become known and my reputation ruined. I played the coward. I did as I was told, for fear of exposure, and because I was surrounded by gunmen who terrified me."

Standing there above the men and women who had suffered for his fault, Herbert Conant snapped off the shackles that had held him for so long and laid bare his soul. But his confession had come too late.

"Get the dirty crook!" A bellowing voice broke off his penitent confession—Then the mob stormed over the porch railing and into the house.

NITA AND Susan Conant were almost overwhelmed by that savage rush. Struggling hopelessly, they were jostled down the steps, thrust into the eager, clawing hands of shrieking women, cursing men. Their screams were a heart-breaking magnet, but the jam about them was so thick that Wentworth and Brackett were almost powerless. For every man they pounded out of their way, a dozen more seemed to materialize. Brackett went down, and then Wentworth was on his knees....

In that supreme moment Herbert Conant mastered the last remnant of his cowardice. Leaping down from the balcony, he landed in the midst of the mob and fought his way doggedly toward his daughter. Half a dozen times he went down—only to struggle back to his feet, face cut and bleeding, clothing hanging from him in rags. Savagely, brutal fists pounded at him, clutching fingers clawed him. He went down again, and that time he did not get up. Kicking and tramping, the mob closed over him, grinding him into the dirt.

Conant had failed to reach his daughter, but his death had not been in vain. His intervention had given Wentworth a breathing space, enabled him to drag Brackett to his feet. Together, they hurled themselves against the crowd, momentarily diverted by the banker's desperate charge, and managed to fight their way to the girls.

Using their guns as clubs, they sprang upon those who held Nita and manhandled Susan Conant, drove them clear and backed the girls against the front of the porch. Grimly, Wentworth leveled his guns.

"You've done enough!" he shouted. "You've beaten the racketeers and driven them out of town. Their leader, Clem Morley, is dead—his body is at police headquarters now. You've killed Conant. That's enough of killing. You've reclaimed your town. Now don't stoop to the level of the thugs you fought, by persecuting these defenseless girls!"

Gradually, his commanding voice and the effect of his personality began to sway them. Richard Wentworth was a born leader, a natural commander—and that crowd sensed his hold on them.

When Ram Singh came riding, as guide, on the running-board of the first carload of state troopers, there was little for the officers to do.

WHEN RICHARD Wentworth limped down the steps of the Harper House the next morning, to where Ram Singh waited at the open door of the Daimler, a grateful crowd of citizens were there to see him off. It was a cheering crowd with gruff Chief Skelly, smiling, at their head. Skelly was more than anxious to have certain little misunderstandings of the past few days forgotten—especially since he had seen the two telegrams now reposing in Wentworth's pocket.

154

One was a message of appreciation of Wentworth's services, and had arrived from the Albany mansion of the governor. The other was an invitation to come in and talk things over with New York's police commissioner, Stanley Kirkpatrick, who had just returned from his European jaunt.

Half an hour before leaving, Wentworth had been closeted with the district attorney. Clifford Brackett had received the prosecutor's assurance that, when his case came to trial, Brackett would receive every possible consideration for his help in downing Willard Kendall and breaking up his lawless reign. Even more important than that to young Brackett was another assurance he had received—the promise that, no matter what he had done, Susan Conant would stand by him.

With a tired smile, Wentworth stepped into the limousine and leaned back against the pillow Nita had propped up behind his wounded shoulder.

"The course is south, Jackson—" he grinned—"back to the peace and quiet of New York!"

Five weeks ago, they had headed north so that Nita might convalesce in rural tranquility—but, after the past week in Harper's Falls, the prospect of Manhattan's crowded streets was strangely appealing. After all, if the Spider had to go on the sick list, where better could he do it than in the throbbing city that was his home?

CAPTAIN COMBAT
❏ #1: The Sky Beast of Berlin $13.95
❏ #2: Red Wings For the Blood Battalion $13.95
❏ #3: Low Ceiling For Nazi Hell Hawks $13.95

OPERATOR 5
❏ #1: The Masked Invasion $13.95
❏ #2: The Invisible Empire $13.95
❏ #3: The Yellow Scourge $13.95
❏ #4: The Melting Death $13.95
❏ #5: Cavern of the Damned $13.95
❏ #6: Master of Broken Men $13.95
❏ #7: Invasion of the Dark Legions $13.95
❏ #8: The Green Death Mists $13.95
❏ #9: Legions of Starvation $13.95
❏ #10: The Red Invader $13.95
❏ #11: The League of War-Monsters $13.95
❏ #12: The Army of the Dead $13.95
❏ #13: March of the Flame Marauders $13.95
❏ #14: Blood Reign of the Dictator $13.95
❏ #15: Invasion of the Yellow Warlords $13.95
❏ #16: Legions of the Death Master $13.95
❏ #17: Hosts of the Flaming Death $13.95
❏ #18: Invasion of the Crimson Death Cult $13.95
❏ #19: Attack of the Blizzard Men $13.95
❏ #20: Scourge of the Invisible Death $13.95
❏ #21: Raiders of the Red Death $13.95
❏ #22: War-Dogs of the Green Destroyer $13.95
❏ #23: Rockets From Hell $13.95
❏ #24: War-Masters from the Orient $13.95
❏ #25: Crime's Reign of Terror $13.95
❏ #26: Death's Ragged Army $13.95
❏ #27: Patriots' Death Battalion $13.95
❏ #28: The Bloody Forty-five Days $13.95
❏ #29: America's Plague Battalions $13.95
❏ #30: Liberty's Suicide Legions $13.95
❏ #31: Siege of the Thousand Patriots $13.95
❏ *NEW:* #32: Patriots' Death March $14.95

DUSTY AYRES AND HIS BATTLE BIRDS
❏ #1: Black Lightning! $13.95
❏ #2: Crimson Doom $13.95
❏ #3: The Purple Tornado $13.95
❏ #4: The Screaming Eye $13.95
❏ #5: The Green Thunderbolt $13.95
❏ #6: The Red Destroyer $13.95
❏ #7: The White Death $13.95
❏ #8: The Black Avenger $13.95
❏ #9: The Silver Typhoon $13.95
❏ #10: The Troposphere F-S $13.95
❏ #11: The Blue Cyclone $13.95
❏ #12: The Tesla Raiders $13.95

MAVERICKS
❏ #1: Five Against the Law $12.95
❏ #2: Mesquite Manhunters $12.95
❏ #3: Bait for the Lobo Pack $12.95
❏ #4: Doc Grimson's Outlaw Posse $12.95
❏ #5: Charlie Parr's Gunsmoke Cure $12.95

THE MYSTERIOUS WU FANG
❏ #1: The Case of the Six Coffins $12.95
❏ #2: The Case of the Scarlet Feather $12.95
❏ #3: The Case of the Yellow Mask $12.95
❏ #4: The Case of the Suicide Tomb $12.95
❏ #5: The Case of the Green Death $12.95
❏ #6: The Case of the Black Lotus $12.95
❏ #7: The Case of the Hidden Scourge $12.95

THE SECRET 6
❏ #1: The Red Shadow $13.95
❏ #2: House of Walking Corpses $13.95
❏ #3: The Monster Murders $13.95
❏ #4: The Golden Alligator $13.95

CAPTAIN ZERO
❏ #1: City of Deadly Sleep $13.95
❏ #2: The Mark of Zero! $13.95
❏ #3: The Golden Murder Syndicate $13.95

www.ingramcontent.com/pod-product-compliance
Lightning Source LLC
Chambersburg PA
CBHW020620250626
47154CB00004B/1593